Hawaiian Legends

OF THE

Guardian Spirits

Hawaiian Legends
OF THE
Guardian Spirits

Retold and Illuminated by
CAREN LOEBEL-FRIED

A Latitude 20 Book

University of Hawai'i Press

HONOLULU

© 2002 Caren Loebel-Fried

All rights reserved

Printed in China

07 06 05 04 03 02   6 5 4 3 2 1

Library of Congress Cataloging-in-Publication Data

Loebel-Fried, Caren.

    Hawaiian legends of the guardian spirits / retold and illuminated by
Caren Loebel-Fried.

       p.   cm.

Summary: A collection of stories that reveal the personal relationship
between the ancient Hawaiian people and all aspects of nature. Includes
notes that explain the historical, cultural, and natural context of the
legends.

    ISBN 0-8248-2537-3 (alk. paper)

    1. Tales—Hawaii. [1. Folklore—Hawaii.] I. Title.

    PZ8.1.L934 Haw 2002

    398.2'09969—dc21

                               2002002822

University of Hawai'i Press books are printed on
acid-free paper and meet the guidelines for permanence
and durability of the Council on Library Resources.

Designed by Argosy

Printed by Palace Press International

To the memory of
Mary Kawena Pukui
who first opened up
the window of understanding for me,
and in gratitude to my husband and son,
who joined me on this journey.

CONTENTS

FOREWORD

by Nona Beamer

Caren Loebel-Fried is a Hawaiian at heart! I am thrilled to feel a soul-sister relationship with her. Her work speaks of the greatness of another Polynesian world, one we will all inhabit with the first perusal of this book. Her writing is fresh and vivid, her artwork strong and alive. My young son, Kaliko Beamer Trapp, and I had the pleasure of assisting with the editorial presentation of the manuscript and found Caren's research to be outstanding. Her attention to detail is wonderful, as her scope embraces not only the philosophical but the spiritual attitudes of Hawaiians.

Hawaiian Legends of the Guardian Spirits will enrich the hearts and minds of readers. You will feel uplifted and fortified with *mana,* the essence of Hawaiian spirituality.

It pleases me and I am honored to write this foreword for Caren. These stories she has retold seem like her very own original creations. The strength of her retelling has come from a very honest wellspring of love for her work on behalf of Hawai'i and its people.

PREFACE

I have always been interested in the legends of the world, particularly those from cultures living at one with nature. Growing up on the New Jersey shore, I spent my childhood exploring the woods around our neighborhood and wandering along the beaches. My mother, a wonderful artist, would carve her woodcuts while my brother and I played in the ocean and sand, and the walls of our home were covered with her graceful prints. One day I would follow in her footsteps, equipped with her old tools and advice, working in the ancient medium of block printing.

As I grew up, I felt increasingly out of step with the culture around me, which distanced itself from nature. My dreams were helpful and in high school I began a dream journal, which I continue to keep. I was interested in the similarities between my dreams and the legends and myths that came from cultures spread across the planet. The ideas of Carl Jung and Joseph Campbell intrigued me. They wrote that all people shared the same unconscious ideas about life, and these archetypal images and motifs could be found in art and mythology. Throughout my life, I have read legends and applied their underlying ideas to my own life, giving me an awareness of that invisible, mysterious realm that underlies our wakeful life experiences, so powerful in the natural world.

It was when I went to Hawai'i for the first time, many years later, that the legends truly came to life for me and I was awakened by the forces of nature there. As I stood on the ground with the active volcano flowing through veins in the earth below, I watched the enchanting birds, the magnificent plants, and the billowing clouds in the sky above. I felt the power and life force of those energies that are personified in the legends. It was a physical experience of what had previously been an intellectual understanding, and it transformed me. I had found my spiritual home. I started reading as many of the legends and myths of Hawai'i as I could get my hands on, and began learning about ancient Hawaiian culture and philosophy. I discovered many beliefs and practices that were familiar to me in my own life, especially the Hawaiian custom of looking for guidance in dreams.

Hawai'i called me back again and again. College studies in anthropology and art came together in my passion for the ancient Hawaiian culture and legends, which offered an unlimited source of inspiration. In 1998 Natalie

Pfeifer, then director of the
Volcano Art Center in
Hawai'i Volcanoes National
Park, proposed that I create a
body of work based on the
guardian spirits, to be
exhibited at the gallery. Thus
began my study of *'aumākua*,
the aspect of Hawaiian
culture that exemplifies the
intimate bond between
people and nature. In the
summer of 2000, I exhibited
a collection of legends and
block prints entitled *Legends
of the Guardian Spirits* in that
magical gallery on top of
Kīlauea. This book has
grown from that exhibit.

    For this volume, I have
selected legends that most
clearly reveal the personal
relationship between the
ancient Hawaiian people and
their ancestors, embodied in
all aspects of nature. My
search for the earliest
versions of the legends brought me to such island resources as
the Bishop Museum Library and Archives in Honolulu. I
explored areas that have histories rich with legends, including
Ka'ū, Hawai'i Volcanoes National Park, the Waipi'o Valley,
Kapoho Bay, North Kohala, and South Kona on the Island of
Hawai'i. In addition, I discovered a wealth of historical
material at the American Museum of Natural History
Research Library in New York City.

    I came upon many variations of the same legends, some
from families in different locales, some told simply and others

with embellishments reflecting the period in which they were recorded. Many versions were written from a European perspective or collected during the missionary period and related through a Christian lens. I have attempted to be as true to the source as possible, referring to the original, archival transcriptions whenever they could be found.

To understand the legends as more than just entertaining stories, one needs some knowledge of their place and purpose in the lives of the people who first told them. Therefore, I included notes that put the legends into context historically, culturally, and within the natural world.

Recently, at an exhibit of old illuminated bibles, I fell in love with the hand-colored woodcuts that graced the pages of those ancient texts. I began experimenting with my own prints, tinting them with colored inks. Besides being great fun to do, I found the colored prints contrasted well with the black-and-white prints, and I was able to bring forth the richness of the beautiful Hawaiian Islands. The color infused the pictures with life and enabled me to more fully express the incredible emotional fire in the legends, as well as my own mythological experience.

And so, within the pages of this volume, I offer these legends of the ʻaumākua as illuminated, sacred texts. I have felt as much an observer as a participant, with the legends and art coming through rather than from me. My goal has been to present the material accurately, while at the same time to communicate to people from many cultures, through words and pictures, the universal themes within the legends. I aim to convey a real feeling for the lives of the ancient Hawaiian people and their personal connection with nature and their ancestors. My hope is that the legends open readers' eyes and hearts to the incredible beauty and power of the natural world and their own connection to it, as Hawaiʻi and the legends have done for me.

ACKNOWLEDGMENTS

Warmest thanks to my editor, Keith Leber, at University of Hawai'i Press for his consistent attention and guidance; to Nona Beamer for her friendship and encouragement, and for helping me "get the feeling right"; to Kaliko Beamer Trapp for critiquing the manuscript; to Patrice Lei Belcher, librarian at the Bishop Museum, for her golden, intuitive recommendations and sharp editorial eye, and for sharing the sacred places from her childhood; to Ron Schaeffer, head of Bishop Museum Archives, and the staff, for their patient detective work; to Ter Depuy, Fia Mattice, and all my friends at Volcano Art Center for their continued support; to Shawn Page and Marc Kinoshita, whose love of the legendary places helped reveal to me the soul of Hawai'i; to Ira Ono, Virginia and Jim Wageman, Aurelia Gutierrez, Stephen Freedman, and Kate Whitcomb for their generosity; to Pudding Lassiter and Amaury Saint-Gilles for their warm welcome; to Mercedes Ingenito, Wendy Wilson, Barbara Koltuv, and Miriam Faugno for their help along the way; and to Natalie Pfeifer for planting the seed. Very special thanks to William Hamilton, director at University of Hawai'i Press; JoAnn Tenorio, design and production manager; and Santos Barbasa, Lucille Aono, and Paul Herr of the Design and Production Department.

Much love and thanks to my husband, Neil, and son, Zack, my mom and Carol, my cousin Julie, my brother, my father and Nancy, my Aunt Bette and Harriet, Kate, Ann Marie, Margaret, Anne, Franca, my twin Sally, the multitude of Frieds, and the rest of my family and friends whose constant belief in the end result helped me to get there. A special *mahalo* to Lucas Baer-Bancroft, Valerie Maxwell, Susan Itkin, Guy Kurshenoff, Ilisa Singer, and Erin Duggan for reading the manuscript.

This book would not have been possible without the research done by those before me, named in the general source list at the back of this volume. I am deeply grateful for their dedication and hard work. Finally, I give my warmest thanks and appreciation to Hawai'i—the islands, the people, the culture, and the legends. *Me ke aloha pumehana.*

INTRODUCTION

Ancient Hawaiians lived in a world where all of nature was alive with the spirits of their ancestors and their gods. Dating back to when the first gods and goddesses arrived in Hawaiʻi, these spirits, called *ʻaumākua*, have lived on through the ages as guardians for their families. *ʻAumākua* take on many natural forms, called *kino lau*, and therefore many Hawaiians are literally related to the animals, plants, and natural phenomena with whom they share the islands. Individuals have a reciprocal relationship with their guardian spirits, offering worship and sacrifice in return for protection, inspiration, and guidance.

Early Hawaiian people did not record their history in books. Instead, they had an oral tradition, and all the great stories were passed on by word of mouth from generation to generation, through legends, myths, prayers, and chants. Therefore, legends were the keepers of history, preserving the Hawaiian culture and traditions. The legends told of the lives of the ancestors, of the exploits of the gods and the chiefs, of fantastic voyages, and of heroic battles. Long chants recorded the genealogies of high-ranking families, connecting them to the creation of the world and to the primary gods. The legends also taught by example how the ancestors lived in their world and how future generations should live in theirs.

People throughout Polynesia and the Pacific share this storytelling tradition. Their legends and myths, often involving the same characters and events, link the various island cultures to a common origin. They also provide clues as to the sea paths the people followed and to the sequence of their exploration and settlement on islands spread wide apart, across thousands of miles of the vast Pacific Ocean.

Although the ancient Hawaiian culture is very different from our own, within the legends we find themes and emotions familiar to us in our modern world. These legends from so long ago come to us as a window through time, where we can catch a glimpse of the lives of the people who first told them. The same energies and stirrings of the spirits that the ancient Hawaiian people felt within the natural world come alive for us today in the legends, and we are given small clues to the meaning that they hold. After reading the legends, we might gaze with new eyes, full of curiosity and wonder, at the great reaching limbs of an old breadfruit tree, or feel a tingle of fear as we hear the cry of the golden plover, circling high in the sky above.

PART ◆ ONE

'Ulu
The Breadfruit

The Gift of Kū

THIS IS THE STORY OF THE GREAT GOD KŪ and his coming to the island of Hawai'i. There was much commotion in the skies with the celebration of Kū's arrival. Sharp flashes of lightning and loud cracks and rumblings of thunder filled the air. The people knew that something unusual was happening, but when he walked into their village, they did not recognize Kū as a god.

Kū lived among the people as a planter. With powerful hands, he moved huge piles of soil effortlessly, and with his 'ō'ō, his long digging stick, he alone did the work of twenty. Alongside the other men who worked this plot of land, Kū planted, weeded, and moved the earth, and his cheerful nature was pleasing to everyone around him.

His strength compared with the other men was enormous. "*E*, Kū! Come now and take a rest!" the men shouted to him when they grew tired. Kū would answer, "'*Ē*, I will in a moment!" The men teased Kū, trying to get him to stop working so they wouldn't seem lazy, but he just kept working. They knew there was something extraordinary about Kū, but the men never imagined he was a god.

His muscular body was a deep, rich brown, attracting the attention of many young women in his *ahupua'a*, the land division where he lived. Sometimes a woman caught sight of him from the *hale kuku*, the house where cloth, called *kapa*, was made by beating the inner bark of the paper mulberry tree. Using her mallet against a wooden anvil, she signaled to the others of Kū's presence with a special, secret rhythm: "Thump, tap-tap, thump, tap-tap. . . . He comes, he comes!" They stole discreet glances at him and sighed, "Kū is so strong and handsome!" But they did not know he was a god.

One day, while walking through the forest valley, Kū happened upon a young woman who was collecting *kukui* nuts from a candlenut tree. The soot from the burnt nuts would be used to print patterns on the beaten *kapa*. She was so busy planning her designs that she did not notice Kū. She sang a little *mele*, a song her *tūtū*, her grandmother, had taught her as a child. With graceful motions, she gathered the nuts, and her sweet voice rose and mingled with the leaves and fragrant flowers around her. Kū was enraptured.

He noticed a dried branch lying across the path and stepped on it to attract her attention. Startled, the young woman looked up, and, recognizing Kū, she smiled warmly. "Aloha, Kū," she said. They talked of the beautiful day, the puffy white clouds in the sky, and the cooling breezes. But as their mouths spoke these words, their eyes and hearts sang of love. Honeycreepers chirped in the surrounding trees and a rainbow spread over them.

Some jealousy greeted the news that Kū and the young woman were going to live as man and wife. "If only *I* had been the one to pick the *kukui* nuts!" said one. But after seeing the couple together, the other women in the village couldn't help but share their happiness. "The heavens must be pleased with this union!" they remarked with pleasure. The couple vowed to build a life together and love one another no matter what might come between them. One day, this promise would be tested.

Over the first few years, Kū's wife admired her husband more and more, marveling at his robust and unceasing energy. Shaking her head and smiling, she told him, "Kū, you have the strength of many men, perhaps even that of a god!" Kū just nodded and said, "And you, my dear wife, you are a goddess to me." Their love for one another grew and grew.

Kū and his wife had two children, a girl and a boy. The children loved and respected their parents and *kūpuna*, their grandparents. Through observation and imitation, the children's days were filled with lessons about living a good life. "They are such happy children," said one neighbor, "and seem to always enjoy helping their parents and grandparents!"

After many years of peace, there came a day when the rains stopped falling. People looked to the dry, cloudless sky with confusion and anxiety. In spite of all their hard work in the fields, the plants started to wither and die. "There must have been some neglect of the gods, some prayers forgotten with the business of digging and planting, some terrible insult unknowingly made!" Their plaintive cries rose up into the sunny sky, but no rain came.

The priest from the neighboring village, a powerful *kahuna*, was called upon to try to appease the anger of the gods. He chanted special prayers and made the proper offerings. But still no rain came. He shook his head and muttered, "It must have been some terrible insult. Maybe things will be better when the rainy season comes. . . ." But they couldn't wait until then. The people would starve!

Kū and his wife watched their own children becoming weak and listless, but what could be done? As all the people looked up at the sky, Kū was gazing down, deep in thought. His face showed the enormous conflict within him. He knew of a way that he could help, but was filled with a profound sadness at what would be lost.

Kū pulled his wife away from the rest of the people. He said, "My wife, I love you and our children with all my heart. There is something that I can do to remedy this situation, but I must go far away."

She looked into his loving eyes, so full of kindness, with a heart heavier than she had ever known before. She turned to look at their children, so tired and listless, and the other people in their extended family, whose shoulders slumped with hopelessness. She saw the barren fields all around them. With sorrow, she finally spoke. "Kū, I have vowed to love you no matter what happens. I will always love you, and now I must let you go."

She collected the children and they followed Kū through the forest to an open field. The air grew heavy, and the surrounding trees were motionless; not the slightest wind blew. Even the birds looked on with silent expectation.

Kū stopped and his family watched him standing there, tall and erect, his feet planted firmly on the land. Gradually he began to sink down into the ground as though the earth were swallowing him up. Soon, all that remained was the top of Kū's head, and his wife wet the soil around him with her tears. The family kept a vigil by the spot where he had buried himself, sitting through the long, sad night, watching and waiting.

With the growing light of early morning, they noticed a slight shifting of the soil where Kū was buried in the earth. A tiny green shoot suddenly sprouted from the spot where Kū's head had been. The family watched with wonder as the plant grew swiftly up and up, branching out as though reaching for every star.

Thousands of shining green leaves unfurled, and soon this magnificent tree was covered with hundreds of 'ulu, the nutritious breadfruit, swinging gracefully from strong branches.

A farmer was walking mournfully through a nearby field, when he suddenly noticed the breadfruit tree in the distance. He let out a cry and ran shouting, "Everyone! Look! Look to the field! Come and see the giant tree where none was before!" The people jumped up with excitement and ran to the tree.

As the people arrived, Kū's wife was sitting under the 'ulu tree with her children standing over her. They formed a great circle around the family. Kū's wife then heard her husband's voice inside her head, and she closed her eyes, listening. He told her, "Wife . . . my body is the trunk of this tree, and my arms are the branches. My hands are the leaves and my head is the fruit. The heart inside each fruit holds the memory of my words. Roast the fruit well, remove the skin, and then you and our children shall eat. . . ."

And so she did.

With excitement, people from the village reached for the 'ulu. But suddenly the entire tree was sucked swiftly back into the ground with a "swoosh." Only when their outstretched hands were lowered did the tree grow back to its full size. A murmur was heard among the crowd, but all became quiet when they saw that Kū spoke to his wife once again.

She heard him say, "Carefully dig up the new shoots around my trunk and share them with our 'ohana and our extended family and friends."

And so she did.

The people planted the sprouts all around their district. These grew just as fast as the first tree had grown, up and up, filling the sky with glistening leaves and plump, ripe fruit. Offshoots from these trees were shared with other friends and family, as well as those in the neighboring ahupua'a, or land division. The breadfruit trees flourished and soon spread across the land, and everyone had 'ulu to eat.

The people thought with awe of the strong, generous man who had lived among them. They now knew that Kū was a god and they would always give thanks to him. They would never again forget to chant the proper prayers or make the appropriate offerings to all the gods and ancestors. They would remember to show how grateful they were to share in the riches of the earth.

And so this was the gift of Kū.

The Sacred Tree

HERE WAS ONCE A SACRED BREADFRUIT tree growing in old Hawai'i. Though it looked like an ordinary tree, it was actually a god, endowed with *mana*, the power to do extraordinary things. But it grew as other trees do, tall and proud, its big green leaves moving this way and that in the gentle trade winds. Many branches hung heavy with fruit, called *'ulu*, which were almost the size and shape of a man's head.

An observant eye might notice that there was something unusual about this tree, for it grew alone in a small, circular clearing. Nearby plants bowed slightly in deference toward it. But no human knew that this breadfruit tree was sacred . . . except for one young woman named Papa.

The sound of waves breaking against coral and lava sang out to Papa, as she sat in the shade plaiting *lau hala*, the dried leaves of the pandanus tree. She lived on a ridge over Kalihi Valley with her husband, Wakea, who had gone into the valley to collect bananas. While Papa worked on new sleeping mats, the song of the sea tickled her imagination, filling her mind with many images.

She pictured the frothy waters left by the surf, undulating like the shadows on the fine mat she was plaiting. The delicate tips of the long, thin leaves she wove wafted in the breeze. They reminded her of the *limu*, the water plants growing on rocks around the tide pools, waving softly in the water. She watched her hands move like busy little crabs.

With every crashing breaker, Papa found it harder to concentrate on her plaiting. She could think only of the treasures that beckoned in the waters below.

"If I am quick," she thought, "I can fetch a delicious surprise for Wakea and be back to my plaiting before he even returns!" Although excited, she was careful to wrap the loose wefts of the mat in round bundles so they wouldn't become tangled. Then she quickly rose and ran down the mountain trail toward the sea with her empty calabash ready to be filled.

The sun through the leaves made speckles of shadow and light on the hard soil beneath Papa's feet as she darted down the rocky path. "Aloha, *'i'iwi!*" she cried to a little red bird whose squeaky voice reached her from a nearby *'ōhi'a* tree growing alongside the trail. She spied him hanging upside down from a branch, his long, curved beak buried deep within a spiky red *lehua* blossom.

Papa finally emerged from the green shadows of the forest. The sun greeted her with a multitude of brilliant jewels spread across the surface of the sea. She stepped slowly onto the warm rocks and sand, catching her breath at the beauty around her.

Then she hurried to the tide pools and started collecting *limu*. She was careful not to disturb the water too much lest she frighten the crabs away into hiding places within the rock crevices. "Ah, these crabs will make a fine meal for Wakea and me!" She plucked one with dexterous fingers from the clear water. Then another and another, until soon the calabash was brimming with her catch. "Now, home I go!" she exclaimed, and disappeared once more into the forest.

Papa carried the full calabash with ease as she made her way up the steep, winding trail. She smiled, imagining the look of surprise on Wakea's face when he discovered her bounty.

At a freshwater spring along the way, she stopped to clean the crabs and *limu*. With cupped hands, she took a deep drink of the cool water. Suddenly, a movement on the mountainside across the valley caught her eye, and Papa squinted through the branches and leaves. She saw a group of men struggling, clutching at someone whose arms were tied behind his back. By their rough handling of this prisoner, she knew the crime must have been serious and that his punishment would be severe.

Suddenly she cried, "Wakea!" The prisoner was her husband! He must have unknowingly taken bananas from the patch that belonged to Leleho'omao, the ruling chief of the area, notorious for his selfishness and cruelty. Papa leaped up, and the delicate flowers fell from the morning glory vine she wore as a skirt. The crabs and plants flew out of her calabash to the ground all around her as she frantically ran down into the valley.

"I must reach them before they hurt or kill Wakea!" she told herself, and urged her feet to move faster. Her heart pounded sharply when she lost sight of them. She must get there in time!

She rushed around a tangled cluster of *hau* trees, covered with bright yellow flowers, opened wide like watchful eyes. On the other side of the thicket, she found herself in front of Wakea and his captors and stopped abruptly.

"Please, let me at least say good-bye to my husband!" Papa pleaded to the men, and they were so startled by her sudden appearance that they nodded their assent.

She grabbed Wakea and held him in a wild embrace. Spinning him round and round, she moved him quickly to a small, circular clearing where a breadfruit tree grew in the center. She pushed Wakea up against the trunk, which opened up wide and then instantly closed around them, the pair disappearing within it.

Dumbfounded, the men rushed up to the tree, grabbing at its trunk and searching through its branches and leaves for the couple. They investigated the surrounding area in angry confusion, but the prisoner and the woman were nowhere to be found. "It is the breadfruit tree!" exclaimed one of the men. "They are hiding inside the trunk. We must chop it down!"

He began hacking at the tree with his stone axe. Bits of bark and wood flew out in all directions. The man shrieked in surprise and pain as the flying chips cut sharply into his flesh, the splattering sap burning and melting away his skin. In agony, he fell to the ground, dead.

The others watched with eyes wide in disbelief, and another man leaped forward, chopping furiously at the trunk of the tree. But he too was struck with the killing wood chips and sap, and quickly fell in a mangled heap beside the first man.

The rest of the men backed away in horror. "We must tell our chief about this tree," said one, and they hurried off to find him.

Chief Leleho'omao was dubious as he listened to the story of the couple's escape. Although he was cruel and selfish, he was not stupid, and he decided that before doing anything, it would be best to consult the *kahuna*, the priest.

After hearing the story, the *kahuna* sat thinking for a while. He eventually raised his head, nodded slowly, and then spoke. "The tree is sacred," he told the chief, "and offerings must be made. Lay coconut and an 'awa root before it, a black pig and some red fish. Before approaching the tree, rub your body well with the oil from a coconut for protection. If you do all that I have told you, then you shall be able to safely cut down this tree."

And so Chief Leleho‘omao and his men brought their offerings to the sacred breadfruit tree, their bodies glistening from head to toe with coconut oil. Hiding his fear, the chief stepped forward with his ax swinging. The other men hesitated, remembering the gruesome scene of the previous day, and watched from a safe distance. As the chief hacked at the tree, they saw he was immune to the flying splinters and sap. They all joined their chief with triumphant cries, and soon the great tree fell. Together, they cleaved the thick trunk until it finally split in two. But where they expected to see their prisoner and his wife, they found solid wood.

Meanwhile, Papa and Wakea had returned to their home, magically transported by the sacred breadfruit tree. Wakea promised Papa that he would be more careful from then on, picking only the fruit from wild groves.

Back in the forest, where Papa's calabash had spilled, the *limu* took root on rocks in the little spring, and there it grows today. The crabs that had scurried from her calabash found new homes in the pool of fresh water where Papa had enjoyed a cool drink. Along the path where Papa ran, wild blue morning glory vines had begun to grow from seeds that had fallen from her skirt that day, the day she saved Wakea, with help from the protective spirit within the sacred breadfruit tree.

NOTES ON THE 'Ulu

Kū and Hina are the great ancestral god and goddess of Hawai'i. The original male and female powers of heaven and earth, they ruled over the fruitfulness of the land and the people. Kū was recognized as the god from whom all gods and people came, and every Hawaiian who lived in the ancient world felt his protection.

Kū was associated with male activities. Early gods of the land and sea were given "Kū" names, and men worshiped the particular Kū god who presided over their profession. There were gods for farming, fishing, war, canoe building, and sorcery, with names like Kūka'ie'ie, Kū'ula, Kūkā'ilimoku, Kūpulupulu, and Kūwahailo.

The word *kū* in Hawaiian means "rising upright, straight," and the breadfruit tree was called *'ulu kū*, or "upright breadfruit." *Ulu* means "to grow, increase, and spread." To the ancient Hawaiians, Kū was the symbol of abundance and so was the breadfruit tree, a *kino lau*, or body form of Kū. Aside from the nutritional value of *'ulu*, the breadfruit tree had many other uses. The trunk made fine surfboards, hula drums, and parts for canoes and houses. The young buds were used as medicine, the inner bark for making *kapa*, or beaten cloth. The sap was used as a caulking material and also smeared on certain tree branches to snare birds in the forest. The birds' valuable feathers were collected to make the cloaks for the *ali'i*, the chiefs. In more modern times, *'ulu* wood was used to make furniture, and the dried buds were burned, the smoke acting as an insect repellent.

According to legend, the first *'ulu* to reach Hawai'i was brought by a man living in Waipi'o named Kaha'i. He voyaged by canoe to his ancestors' ancient homeland in *kahiki* (the name for a foreign land) and brought back the *'ulu*, which he planted at Puʻuloa in ʻEwa, a sacred area on the southwest coast of Oʻahu. The actual date of the breadfruit tree's arrival to Hawaiʻi is uncertain, but many clues point to some time after the fourteenth century. The place of origin is thought to be Malaysia; from there it spread to the southern islands of Polynesia and then to Hawaiʻi.

The breadfruit does not often reproduce from seeds but from shoots growing at the base of the tree. Early Hawaiians described ʻulu with the expression ʻai kamehaʻi, meaning it is food that reproduces itself "by the will of the gods." To transplant a sucker, one must cut the parent root at just the right place, keeping a ball of soil intact around the root. The root must be planted carefully in rich, dark soil, not sand or cinder, then mulched and watered frequently in order for the progeny to survive and flourish. Considering the difficulty of this procedure, the success that early voyagers had with transplanting the ʻulu is almost as magical as the legends themselves.

PART TWO

Kōlea

The Plover

A Warning from the God of the Plover

KUMUHANA LOVED THE TASTE OF plovers, the small birds with the golden-flecked feathers known as *kōlea* in Hawai'i. He hunted at night and caught them while they slept, filling his net with hundreds of birds, many more than one man could possibly eat.

Over his fire Kumuhana roasted the *kōlea*, stuffing two at a time into his greedy mouth with fingers black and greasy from the charred carcasses. He gorged himself and fell asleep when he could eat no more. And as he snored, a pile of uneaten plovers lay atop the hot coals, sizzling through the night until all that remained were ashes.

Night after night, Kumuhana's cooking fire blazed. As the *kōlea* roasted, smoke billowed up over his house and drifted to the house next door, where there lived a man who worshipped the god of the plover. When this poor man inhaled the defiling smoke, he became violently ill, doubled over in pain. He knew Kumuhana's excesses were an intolerable insult to his god, but what could be done? Clutching his cramped stomach, he would cry, "*Auwē, Auwē!* Alas! I pray to thee, god of the plover! I am sorry for the disrespect shown to you by Kumuhana. Please, help me convince him to change his ways. Send me your guidance!"

One evening, the two men met in the clearing between their houses while Kumuhana was on his way to catch *kōlea*. At that moment, a plaintive cry broke through the red clouds above: "Chaleeeee!"—the call of the golden plover. Both men looked up, and the neighbor paled. With grave concern he said, "Take heed, Kumuhana, for that is a warning to you from the god of the plover!"

Kumuhana snorted and spoke with contempt. "Perhaps it is for you that this message comes, for *I* do not worship *your* bird-god!" And with that, Kumuhana sauntered off into the setting sun, his net slapping against his back with each step. The neighbor watched and, shaking his head, whispered solemnly, "Oh, god of the plover, he does not listen."

Within the gray twilight, Kumuhana crept quietly through the shadows toward the birds' roosting place, where he found many plovers sleeping peacefully on the rocks. Wasting no time, he started to capture them, quickly filling his net with the small, defenseless creatures. Soon, the net could hold no more and hung heavy on his back as he ambled home. He hardly noticed, for he reveled in anticipation of his coming meal. With his mouth watering and big belly rumbling, he breathed, "How I love the taste of plovers!"

But when he arrived at his house, the net suddenly felt as light as a feather. "How strange!" he said, and drew the net around, laying it on the ground before him. There he found not a remnant of their golden plumage; all of the birds were gone!

Certain that his neighbor was responsible, he cried, "I will get my *kōlea* back, even if I have to kill that man," and he charged to the man's house. But when confronted with the theft, his neighbor was obviously mystified. "I have not taken your *kōlea!*" he said. "But what is that sound coming from your house?"

Kumuhana turned and the sound that he heard made the hair on his neck stand up: the roar of thousands of wailing plovers. Confused and angry, Kumuhana spat, "So, you think you can fool with me?" and he raced to his house. His neighbor cried out, "Say a prayer to the god of the plover, before it is too late!" But his words were carried away like smoke in the wind.

When Kumuhana reached the entrance of his house, the racket from inside suddenly ceased. He stopped, and a chill of fear swept over him. Cautiously leaning over the threshold, he peeked inside. The room was dim and eerily silent. As his eyes adjusted to the gloom, he found the room was filled with black pebbles, piled from the floor all the way up to the windows. He shook his head slowly with disbelief, mumbling, "This must be some sort of prank. . . ." But then the pebbles seemed to be moving. He squinted his eyes, looking hard, for the strange mass now seemed not to be pebbles at all, but birds, thousands of *kōlea*. Writhing and wriggling, with shining black eyes staring at him, they shook out their gleaming, gold-flecked feathers. Kumuhana stood like a statue in the entrance, paralyzed by the astonishing sight before him.

And then the birds were upon him. Pecking his eyes, tearing at his flesh with small, needle-sharp claws, they overwhelmed him with their numbers. Kumuhana shrieked. Blind and bleeding, he waved his arms madly, trying to shake off the furious mob, but his hands swept right through their ghostly bodies. He staggered outside, struggling under the throng of screeching plovers, and stumbled right into his cooking fire, which now mysteriously blazed. The flames engulfed him, rising high into the air. Kumuhana screamed, but no one heard, for his voice was lost amid the deafening roar of thousands of *kōlea* crying, "Chaleeeeeeeeeeeeeee!"

And so the life of Kumuhana was lost that night, taken by the very birds he had so ruthlessly slaughtered. People from the village shook their heads, saying, "*E*, Kumuhana has only himself to blame. It was his greedy and wasteful habits that did him in." His neighbor felt sympathy for Kumuhana, but knew that disrespect shown to a god, even a god that belonged to another, had its consequences. Gazing at the pile of sooty ashes left in Kumuhana's fireplace the next morning, he murmured, "Unfortunate for Kumuhana that he did not heed the warning from the god of the plover."

NOTES ON THE Kōlea

Pacific golden plovers, called *kōlea*, leave their breeding grounds in Siberia and Alaska during late summer and fly 3,000 miles to Hawai'i. These incredible birds maintain an average speed of 60 miles per hour, their nonstop journey over the sea taking nearly two days and nights. Helped by strong seasonal winds, they use the stars, the position of the sun, and possibly the Earth's magnetic field to find their way. The three-month-old fledglings, which have never seen Hawai'i, make the trip nearly a month after the adults have gone, somehow finding their own way to the islands.

Though their plumage changes colors seasonally, Pacific golden plovers are named for the beautiful golden flecks on their back feathers. The birds can be found throughout Hawai'i during fall, winter, and spring, feeding on crustaceans along the shoreline or searching for insects and berries on lawns, fields, and grassy mountain slopes. When summer approaches, the plovers once again take to the air, beginning the long journey back to their breeding grounds in the north.

Ancient Polynesian voyagers in search of land may have followed migrating *kōlea* flying high overhead. Ever observant of the plovers' transient ways, Hawaiian people have used the *kōlea* as a metaphor. An independent person prone to wandering, for example, is compared to the *kōlea*. Noting that the plover's body is lean when it arrives and fat when it departs from Hawai'i's shores, another proverb likens the *kōlea* to those people who come to the islands to make their fortune and then take it back home with them.

Early Hawaiians netted plovers for food, but killing the birds wastefully was not approved of, and one who called the *kōlea* his guardian spirit would never eat or harm a plover. In ancient Hawai'i, most people looked upon these intriguing birds as spirit beings. The oldest legends tell of plovers acting as intermediaries, carrying messages from the gods to the people. A *kōlea* circling over a house, uttering its eerie cry, was viewed as an omen of death. The legend of Kumuhana and his acts of disrespect toward plovers are still remembered, for the place where he lived and died is called 'Aiākōlea, which means irreverence to the plover.

PART ◆ THREE

Manō

The Shark

Legend of the Little Green Shark
The Journey

HE MAN SAT WITH PERFECT STILLNESS on the double canoe, his body one with the rolling body of the vessel, as though both were carved from the same wooden log. He was the principal navigator on board, the one responsible for finding the way across this vast open sea, and he followed a star path that had been blazed by those who sailed before him. Powered by wind, the vessel rolled on toward Hawai'i, its hulls like the torsos of two great sharks, plowing through the dark sea beneath a blue-black sky radiant with stars.

Gazing up to read the information contained in the sky, the navigator squinted, for his eyes were tired and stinging. The stars, moon, and planets spoke to him, and he felt messages in the graceful ocean swells. Referring to notches carved into the side rails of the vessel, he double-checked to see how they lined up with the stars on the horizon and in the great dome of the sky above him. "Yes," he said, "we are on course." But then he frowned. Could he trust his reading of the stars and the currents? At the start of the journey, his mind had been sharp and alert, but now he felt sluggish and slow from so many nights of little sleep. Even a slight miscalculation would be catastrophic, causing them to miss their target on this journey across these 3,000 miles of open sea.

The night was quiet but for the splashing of the waves against the hulls and the whistle of the wind caught in the huge sails of woven pandanus leaves above him. He glanced up at their sharp forms, so much like massive fins rising into the sky. The rope lines slapped softly against the tall, wooden masts, lulling the tired man. His mind began to drift like the flotsam that floated by the canoe, and the navigator's thoughts were filled with colorful memories of his homeland in Tahiti and how this great voyage began.

There was much unrest in the land of Tahiti. Chief Tua, a kind and intelligent ruler, was a great warrior and had been successful at fighting off the enemies bordering on his district. But attacks were coming more frequently, and word had reached him that a new enemy was fast approaching. Chief Tua yearned for a life of peace, for himself and his people.

One night he had a dream. In this dream was a vision of the island of Hawai'i. A beautiful, fertile land this was, whose inhabitants were friendly and welcoming. Tua's ancestral spirits spoke to him, telling him, "Go, Tua! Now is a propitious time to venture forth to this new land!" And so, in the morning, he gathered his favorite sister and male relatives who lived in his district. The navigator was among them.

Chief Tua told them of his dream. "Come with me to Hawai'i!" he said. "We will be leaving behind Tahiti, where our family has lived for generations. But we can no longer live here in peace. In the stories told by those who traveled there before us, Hawai'i is a productive and welcoming land. So let us go and start a new life there!" They were all tired of their struggles in Tahiti and eager to join Tua. They were, after all, a seafaring people, skilled in the building and sailing of canoes. It was decided that they would begin the preparations at once.

Four
double-
hulled canoes
were to be built.
Each artisan was a
specialist in his particular
tradition, having obtained his knowledge
from years of study with an expert in the
field. All the work was undertaken with
strict attention paid to the gods, and
proper procedures were painstakingly
adhered to. The master canoe designer
had spent three days in the deep forest
before selecting the trees that would
become the hulls. The priest, with
prayers and offerings, had blessed the
trees before they were felled. From
the rough carving to the shaping
and fine finishing, the oars and
all the wooden parts were
crafted using tools
of stone and
bone.

Master craftswomen picked and dried pandanus leaves, then carefully plaited enormous mats for the sails. Finally, after six months of labor, all the parts were assembled and lashed together, and the finishing work was done. Four magnificent vessels stood tall and proud, each equipped with a small projection at their stern, the seat where the ancestral spirit would ride.

The people were well practiced in the provisioning of canoes for a long voyage. They brought on board gourds filled with fresh water, and many fruits and vegetables for the start of the journey. For the remainder of the trip, they had preserved and carefully wrapped dried fish and fermented taro, yam, breadfruit, banana, sweet potato, and coconut. Any fish caught along the way would supplement this nutritious diet, and supplies of fresh water for drinking could be replenished with rainwater collected off the sails.

They were also bringing along many plants to cultivate in their new homeland.

The tubers, cuttings, and young offshoots were all packaged well so they would survive the time at sea. These bundles now hung safely in grass shelters on the canoe decks, protected from the ocean's destructive salty sprays. The chickens, pigs, and dogs they brought on board would adapt well to their new home, so similar to the one they were leaving behind.

Dreams had been analyzed throughout the preparations for the journey, for this was sacred work and dreams were the communications of the gods. All the signs pointed to a successful voyage.

And so, finally, they were ready to embark on their journey. On the night before they were to sail, Chief Tua slept inside one of the big hulls of the canoe on which he was to travel, imbuing the great vessel with power. With the rise of the navigation star the next morning, the crew was ready to set sail. The navigator joined Chief Tua, his sister, the steersmen, the priests, the astrologer, the prophet, the poet, the paddlers, and the director of the winds, all of them ready for this voyage to a new life in the beautiful land of Hawai'i.

Now, after so many weeks at sea, it was early morning and the sky was just beginning to grow pale. The navigator gazed at the

other canoes around him, dark shapes tossing in the gentle waves, and he felt a pang of worry. His responsibility to all the people on board these vessels was weighing heavily upon him. Would he soon see the island's volcanic profile rising from the sea? Would the gods answer his prayers for a successful journey?

He scanned the dim horizon and noticed a cumulus cloud, the type of cloud that only forms over a landmass. Watching the cloud, he saw a bird flying toward the canoe from that same direction and quickly identified the noddy tern, known to nest on island coastal cliffs and fly out to sea for a morning meal. With growing excitement, he located a star glowing faintly just above the cloud, the zenith star of Hawai'i. All of his observations answered to his longing, and now he knew for certain. He whispered, "We are here!"

With passion, he started to sing a *mele*, or song of celebration, composed by a navigator who had sailed on this same star path, across this vast, wide ocean before him:

Behold Hawai'i, an island, a people!
The people of Hawai'i
Are the children of Tahiti!*

The *pū*, the great spiral conch shell, was blown to gather all the canoes together, and its deep moan resonated far out over the churning sea. All of the people now gazed at the great volcanic island rising from the depths, relief and gladness filling their hearts now that their voyage was finally nearing its end.

The canoes were still too far away for Tua's family to notice the people gathered at the shore. These were the people of Hawai'i, who saw their world as poetry. They watched the distant canoes with sails of shark fins cutting through the waves, a band of warriors on their horizon. But they were not afraid; instead they were joyful, for this was the coming of the gods.

And little did Chief Tua and his family realize what legends would later be told of this journey from Tahiti to their new home in Hawai'i.

---

*From a chant composed by Kamahu'alele, an ancient navigator, on sighting Hawai'i at the end of a voyage back from Tahiti.

Legend of the Little Green Shark
The Coming of the Sharks

O Ka'ū of the rumbling earth!
Where verdant forests of the uplands bring forth ferns
    and maile vines,
Watered with rainfalls and cold mists sent on the breezes
    by majestic Mauna Loa.
O Nā'ālehu, sloping gracefully above the sea,
Where fertile red earth brings forth sweet potatoes, sugar cane,
    and bananas,
And rolling plains sprout tufts of tall pili grasses.
O Waikapuna of the windy shore,
Where tumbling waves meet the white sandy beach,
And powerful currents bring forth 'ahi tuna, bonito, mackerel,
    and ulua, the jack.*

---

*A mele, or chant, composed by the author, written in the style of
ancient Hawaiian chants, based on the history of the families from
Ka'ū.

The storyteller paused and all were silent. The audience of men, women, and children sat rapt with attention, perfectly still, for any movement would show disrespect for the gods.

With arms, hands, and fingers moving expressively through the air, describing the images he chanted, the man continued:

Wake now, sleepy cloud that billows plump in the sky above the sea!
The early morning sun colors you a golden orange.
A salty breeze blows gently in from the sea over the rocky shore,
And the beach is embraced by a lei of blue morning glories.
But now, look forth to the horizon where clouds brush the water!
So many sharp points of light do appear.
Are these just waves, or the sails of many canoes,
Catching the first rays of sunshine?
Are these fierce warriors from Kahiki, a distant land?
O, the sea brings forth a multitude of manō!
Shark fins weave through dark choppy waters like jagged
*   mountain peaks,*
Like mighty sails on four double canoes cutting through the waves,
Majestic and proud, they approach our shore!
Look forth to Kua!* Ke Aliʻi Manō, great Chief of the Sharks,
O, Kua of the thick skin, red like the blossoms of the wiliwili tree,†
Look forth to Kua's sister! Upon his back the woman rides,
Tall and strong, she is a guiding star,

---

*In Hawaiʻi, the letter *t* was replaced by the letter *k*; therefore Chief Tua from Tahiti was called Kua.
†A Hawaiian proverb says that when the *wiliwili* tree blooms its red blossoms, the shark bites. The color red is also associated with the gods.

Navigating through rough waters in the dark of night,
Together they lead this great band of warriors to Hawai'i.

Everyone in the audience was leaning forward, excitement showing in their sparkling eyes. Not even a whisper was heard from the trees as everyone waited.

    The storyteller then took a slow breath and continued his melodious chant of this legend, this *mo'olelo* of Kua, the Great Red Shark.

The island trembled, thunder cracked and peeled,
And long clouds hung low on the horizon beneath the sun.
But a rainbow* spread high across the breezy sky,
And so, we greeted them in friendship,
With aloha, we welcomed them to our land.
Striding ashore was Kua, with friendship in his heart.

---

*Rainbows appeared when gods and chiefs were present.

Among us he mingled and in spirit form he married,
A woman from our family becoming his wife.
She was fresh like the first tender flower of a milo tree.
From their union was brought forth a human girl,
And a little green shark called Pakaiea.
Kua's sister married one of our own proud chiefs,
Becoming ancestress to our people.
And so the generations followed,
Of manō and kānaka, sharks and humans, bonded by blood,
    spirit, and love.
O Kua, we are strong with your blood flowing through our veins,
"Na mamo i ka halo o Kua," we are the children of the bosom
    *of Kua.**
This is known.

Then, changing his tone, the storyteller said, "And so, my friends, thus began our *'ohana*, our family, all descendants of Kua, the Great Red Shark."

Everyone sat back with a sigh of satisfaction, eyes bright and heads nodding, for this gifted storyteller had chanted well this great story of their ancestors.

---

*Said by Ka'ū residents, who considered themselves ancestors of Kua, the Great Red Shark, as quoted in *The Polynesian Family System*, by Handy and Pukui, p. 36.

Legend of the Little Green Shark
The Birth of Pakaiea

HERE WAS A YOUNG WOMAN WHO lived with her parents in Ka'ū, at the southern tip of Hawai'i, off the sandy shore. A gentle young woman she was, "fresh like a *milo* blossom," her family would lovingly say of her. Her days were busy, filled with the crafts she learned from her mother and grandmother, the plaiting of baskets from *hala* leaves, and the spinning of cordage out of coconut fibers. She helped care for the children in their family, those too small to care for themselves. By nightfall she was always exhausted and slept deeply.

One night she dreamed of a tall, powerful man who came to her from the sea. His dark, muscled body moved slowly, smoothly toward her, his strong shoulders tattooed with the symbols of sharks. With the sound of waves gently caressing the shore, the man tenderly touched her face and hair, and the two became lovers.

In the morning, while cleaning the *hale noa,* or sleeping house, she was consumed by the memory of her dream, every detail so vivid in her mind. Noticing how distracted and forgetful the young woman was, her mother approached her, and the dream was revealed. Her mother was concerned, because dreams might be messages sent by the gods or the ancestors, so she rushed to tell the young woman's father.

Later in the morning, he saw his daughter kneeling by the seashore picking *limu,* or water plants, from the rocks. A short distance away, he hid himself behind a rough wall of lava and watched her closely. He noticed her head moving this way and that as she scanned the ocean, and he became very suspicious. "She is looking for this man, who must have come during the night by canoe!"

That night he kept a vigil outside of the hut where she slept. He sat quiet and still, squinting through the darkness for signs of a visitor, straining to hear the sound of feet striding up the ocean path. But all through the night, no one appeared. Out of the hut came his daughter with the rising of the sun, and she told her father that the dream had come again, the dream of the man from the sea.

Night after night the dreams continued. Her parents soon realized that their daughter's nightly visitor was an *akua manō,* a shark god, because eventually the young woman became pregnant. One day she gave birth to a baby shark. She took the baby down to the shore and carefully wrapped him in *pakaiea,* a green seaweed with red markings. Calling out to the shark god to come for his son, she gently placed the little baby shark in the water.

After many weeks, the spirit of the *manō* one day appeared and spoke to the family through a *haka*, or medium. "I am Pakaiea, the little green shark," he said, "named after the seaweed that my mother wrapped me in at birth. Please, my family, do not call upon me unless you are in dire need, and only worship me at such times. Take care never to eat the flesh of a shark or the type of seaweed that bears my name, for this

would be an insult to me. Always remember, if you need me I will be nearby, in the ocean watching over you."

Many years and generations passed. One day a descendant of the woman, a man named Kahikina, was out fishing under a sunny sky in the waters off Ka'ū. Suddenly there was a crash, and his canoe lurched sideways. Terrified, Kahikina held tight to the sides, and he watched as a massive shark came at the canoe and rammed his head fiercely into the small vessel. "A man-eater!" he cried. Kahikina knew that this *manō* would make a meal of him if he could. He shouted prayers to Kanaloa, god of the sea, as he struck at the enemy shark with his paddle. Unshaken, the beast rushed in again with a vengeance.

Kahikina noticed his feet were getting wet and he glanced down anxiously to see water coming in through the cracked side, starting to fill the bottom of the vessel. Looking up, his heart suddenly caught in his throat, for in the waters just ahead was another shark fast approaching. Panicked, he raised his paddle high, preparing to fight off this new foe. But to his amazement, instead of attacking the canoe, the smaller, green-colored creature charged at the man-eater. Relentlessly thrashing with fins and tail, the little green shark did not stop until the larger shark was driven away. Then the little shark swam under the canoe and towed it all the way back to shore.

Kahikina stepped onto dry land and turned to see who it was that had rescued him. He immediately realized it was Pakaiea, whose beautiful sleek skin bore the green and red markings of the seaweed after which he was named.

"Pakaiea!" he cried to the *manō*. "You saved my life!" The little green shark swam slowly in the shallow waters, his bright eyes watching Kahikina. The man hurried home to collect bananas and *'awa* root, from which the drink of the gods is made, and brought them to the shark as an offering of thanks.

They remained great friends ever after, with Kahikina the *kahu*, or keeper, of the little green shark, responsible for his care and worship. Pakaiea helped Kahikina to become a successful fisherman, driving schools of fish into the man's awaiting nets, and the first of the catch was always given to the shark. The man prepared special foods for his guardian every day. He would cook potatoes, *kalo* (taro), bananas, and sugarcane with reverence and place the food in gourd containers slung in nets off both ends of a carrying stick. Bringing these offerings to the shore, he would call out, "Pakaiea!" and the little green shark always appeared. Kahikina fed the shark and tenderly cleaned barnacles off his back.

Many years passed until the day came when Kahikina had become a very old man. As he walked slowly to the beach, struggling under the weight of the full gourds he carried, his heart grew heavy. When he reached the shore, he called out to his *manō,* and as the shark arrived at the water's edge, Kahikina knelt down beside him. Speaking quietly to the little green shark, he said, "We have been good friends for a long time, but I am getting too old to care for you. My son will soon become your *kahu,* your keeper."

Pakaiea's eyes shone from just above the water line, bright with understanding and compassion. After a while, the little green shark turned and swam slowly away. Kahikina watched as the shark's fins mingled and soon disappeared within the sharp whitecaps dancing across the surface of the evening sea.

How he loved his wonderful guardian and friend Pakaiea! And the sea, how it filled him with awe, with its power and mystery, the great provider for him and his family through the generations, throughout the ages. Across this vast ocean long ago, his voyaging ancestors had set a course for Hawai'i from Tahiti. Kahikina felt at one with this *ʻāina,* the land, and this *moana,* the grand, vibrant sea. He felt within himself the spirits of his ancestors, whom he would soon be among, and all the gods who lived on through the plants, animals, and elements around him. Kahikina was brimming with aloha for this great *ʻohana,* his family, all part of the earth and the sea.

And he sighed.

Notes on the Manō

The navigation skills of the ancient Polynesians that enabled them to explore thousands of miles of the vast Pacific Ocean have captured the modern imagination. Without the help of metal, machinery, compasses, or printed maps, these sailors built canoes and voyaged over huge distances of open ocean. Their navigators learned and committed to memory the patterns of stars and planets in the sky, the currents, and the many other clues nature provided. They returned to their homeland to share with others the knowledge and experience they had collected. The voyages continued, back and forth, and many islands were discovered and settled.

Much of our knowledge of these early voyages comes from legends and myths. They were passed down through the generations by elders and by gifted storytellers with exceptional memories, whose chanting of the stories sometimes took days to complete. Within the chanted stories, metaphors were often used to describe people and events. For instance, warriors sailing a fleet of canoes might be referred to as a band of sharks. At the same time, it was believed that the spirit of an ancestor lived on in many body forms, called *kino lau,* such as within the body of a shark. So in a legend a shark ancestor could be both a symbolic portrayal of an ancestral warrior and a factual description of a shark who was related to a person by blood.

There are many accounts in Hawai'i in which the lives of sharks and people are intertwined. Not all sharks were *'aumākua,* or guardian spirits; many sharks were known as man-eaters. Unlike other guardians, sharks were worshipped and cared for as individuals, called by name and recognized by their distinct coloring, features, and behavior. There were special patron sharks, famous in a particular location, who would provide to their devotees protection from man-eaters and an abundant catch for fishermen. Many stories are told of *manō kānaka*, or guardian sharks, who rescued shipwrecked people and conveyed them to shore on the sharks' backs, sometimes even fanning the waters to keep the people warm.

People who were related to sharks had to be very careful to follow the specific *kapu*, or sacred laws, concerning their guardians. If they were to eat the flesh of a shark, their stomachs would become swollen, distended, and horribly painful. Consuming certain types of seaweed associated with the shark would cause sores in the mouth. Since these conditions were a result of an insult to the guardian spirit, relief would only come through prayers and offerings, with the help of a priest. If the apology was accepted, the person's health would be restored.

The Legend of the Little Green Shark describes the interdependent relationship between humans and sharks, and illustrates how the ancient Hawaiians looked on a potentially dangerous animal as a trusted member of the family. The familial bond with the shark is still a reality, with many contemporary Hawaiians living as their ancestors did, in communion with their ancestral guardians. They continue to experience nature as a world infused with consciousness, all part of one *ʻohana*, one family.

PART FOUR

Ipu
The Gourd

Twins of the Gourd

ANY YEARS AGO, IN KAMĀʻOA, KAʻŪ, ON the Big Island of Hawaiʻi, there lived a young chiefess who died while pregnant. Her family and the people of the village were stricken with grief, for they had loved her dearly. During ten days of mourning, the air was filled with their anguished cries of lamentation and chanted eulogies. Her husband laid her body to rest in a burial cave and rolled a big stone before the entrance, disguising the opening.

Unbeknownst to her husband, a gourd vine sprouted from the dead woman's navel on the day she was due to give birth. Along the rocky floor it grew, winding its way out of the cave's opening and around the big stone. The thick green vine meandered west over miles of the Kamāʻoa plain, creeping through many districts, its giant leaves shiny and robust. Finally, when it had reached the border of Kona, a crisp white flower sprouted at the end of the vine. A day later, the flower withered and fell to the ground, leaving in its place a tiny *ipu*, or gourd.

The gourd grew in a field next to where a fisherman lived. While gazing out from his hut one afternoon, he noticed the little gourd and, filled with curiosity, walked out to take a closer look. A smile spread over his face as he approached and he cried, "Just look at this beautiful *ipu!* What a fine gourd you are! If I nurture you well, you will grow to be huge and round, and will make a perfect container for all of my fishing gear!"

He went immediately to collect three sticks, constructing a frame to support the *ipu* so it would not flatten on the bottom as it grew heavier. He removed small stones from beneath the fruit and made a cushion of grass on the ground for the gourd to rest on. He made many tiny adjustments before he was satisfied.

And so the fisherman cared for the gourd, and as the weeks and months passed, it grew large and round. One evening, while on his daily inspection, the fisherman noticed that the gourd's vine had started to dry out and shrink. Kneeling beside it, he struck the big gourd sharply a few times, listening carefully. "Thump, thump, thump." It made a low, dull sound. "No," he said, "you are not ripe yet, but soon!" He pinched and squeezed the *ipu* just to make certain that it was not ready to harvest. Then he propped it carefully again inside the frame, admiring its perfect round shape before returning to his hut.

That very night, the spirit of the chiefess came to her husband in a dream. She looked miserable and complained of being pinched, thumped, and bruised. She told him, "Go and find the *ipu*. You must bring it back home!"

When the husband awoke the next morning, his wife's face and words were vivid in his mind, and he hurried to the cave where she was buried. His heart beat furiously when he discovered the gourd vine growing out of the cave's small opening, and he crawled inside to find its source. He stopped short at the sight of his wife's lifeless body, with the living vine growing from her, so healthy and full of vitality. He fell to his knees before the dead woman, crying passionately, "Yes, my darling wife, I will find your *ipu*!"

He set off at once. Following the winding, leafy plant westward, he walked many miles, through seven districts over the Kamā'oa plain, until finally he came upon the gourd. He picked up the plump, beautiful fruit and cradled it in his arms with great sadness and longing. As his wife had instructed in the dream, he prepared to remove the gourd from its long vine and bring it home.

The fisherman happened to be looking out of his hut when he spied the stranger behind his house holding the gourd. He ran out to the man shouting, "Put that gourd down! It belongs to me!"

He grabbed at the gourd fiercely, trying to pull it away. The husband cried, "Please, stop! Listen to me! This gourd is sacred!" The fisherman dropped his arms, breathing hard with indignation and confusion. The husband said quietly, "I can explain."

He told the fisherman his sad story, all the while rocking the gourd gently, like a baby. By the time the husband finished speaking, the fisherman's anger had turned to compassion. He said, "'Ae, the gourd belongs to you, and you can be sure that through all these months I have cared for it well."

The husband graciously thanked the fisherman and started the long walk home, speaking softly to the *ipu* all along the way. When he finally arrived, it was dark. He wrapped the gourd in a soft piece of *kapa*, bark cloth, and went immediately to sleep, exhausted after the day's toil.

In the morning he woke up slowly and felt groggy. But then, remembering the adventures of the day before, he leapt up from his sleeping mats and hurried to the gourd. Carefully unwrapping the *kapa*, he found that the *ipu* had cracked open during the night. And there, within the folds of the soft cloth, lay two seeds.

His heart overflowed with gladness as he envisioned the marvelous plants and the multitude of gourds that would grow from these two seeds. He held them carefully, preparing to store them away until the rainy season, when he felt them quiver ever so slightly. Startled, he looked carefully at the two seeds. Sure enough, they moved again, and suddenly, to the man's amazement, from each seed sprang a tiny baby girl.

He watched with awe as the miniature babies swiftly grew bigger and bigger, until they reached the size of normal infants, filling his arms with their warm softness. He held the identical twin girls tenderly, touching his cheek to each of their heads. With tears filling his eyes he whispered, "My wife, this gift from you and the gods is a joy to me. I will care for our daughters, raise them, and protect them."

The years passed and the girls grew up healthy and strong under their father's loving care. They soon matured into fine, strong women, with the chiefly blood of their mother running through their veins. Eventually, they married and became mothers of many children.

As the years and generations passed, the family spread westward over the Kamāʻoa plain, settling on the same land that the gourd vine had once crept across. Over time, their population grew, and the twins became ancestors to thousands. Members of the family called themselves the Children of the Gourd, and the memory of their origin was kept alive with the telling of this legend. The sacred *ipu* remained a guiding force to the people of the Kamāʻoa plain forever after.

Notes on the Ipu

The Hawaiian word for gourd, *ipu,* is also the name for a container or vessel. A symbol of abundance for early Hawaiian people, gourds grew in various shapes and sizes and were cultivated for many different uses. The dryness of the Kamāʻoa plains made the carrying and storing of fresh water essential. The gourd made a perfect water container and could also be used as a calabash for storing food, dishes, hula drums, fishing gear, and *kapa,* or bark cloth. Gourds were suspended in woven nets, hung balanced on both sides of a shoulder pole for carrying over long distances.

One whose *ʻaumakua* was the *ipu* would place a gourd by the head of a pregnant woman during a difficult labor so the

ancestor could help with the delivery. Gourd fragments and dried vines were *kapu,* or sacred, and never burned by family members, for they were considered to be the bones of an ancestor. Instead, they would be buried in a deep hole. To keep others from stealing a prized gourd growing on the vine, the family would give it an ancestor's name, letting everyone know that this gourd was sacred and not to be touched.

The *ipu* was a body form of
Lono, one of the four primary
gods of Hawai'i. Known as
the Provider, Lono was a
nourishing god associated with
rain clouds, growth, and the
harvest. In the *Pule Ipu,* or
Prayer of the Gourd, chanted
during the ritual when a boy
became a man, the world was
described as a great gourd, its
handle a rainbow and its lid the
heavens, containing the
multitude of gods. With its full,
round shape, so much like a
womb, the gourd on the vine
contained the seeds of creation,
and in early Hawai'i, the *ipu*
was used to hold all the
necessities of life.

PART ◆ FIVE

Pueo

The Owl

The Seven Eggs

ONG AGO IN KAHEHUNA ON THE ISLAND of Oʻahu, there lived a man named Kapoʻi. He was a simple, quiet man who took care only of himself, for he had never married. Though getting on in years, Kapoʻi was still in good health, nimble in his muscles and mind, and satisfied with his life. He nurtured the plants in his small garden, caught a few fish to eat with his poi, and kept his little thatched hut tidy and well maintained.

In nearby Waikīkī lived Kākuhihewa, the paramount chief of Oʻahu. He was a fair and beloved ruler, but he dealt with any perceived wrongdoing severely. When he defeated an enemy in war, Chief Kākuhihewa had a life-size wooden carving made to look exactly like the beaten man, bent over on his hands and knees in a position of humiliating subservience. Platters of food were served atop these wooden figures, from which the king ate with zeal. Kapoʻi did not want to anger his ruler, so he did all that he could to follow the laws and avoid trouble.

One night, just before falling off to sleep, Kapoʻi felt a drop of rain hit him on the head. He had noticed that his roof was a little windblown, but had not realized how loose it had become. He grunted and turned himself around so he faced the other direction. "I will have to make the repairs tomorrow," he told himself. The rain was light and soon stopped, and he had a good night's sleep.

The next morning, Kapoʻi awoke refreshed and ready for the new day. After a light meal, he went off at once to Kewalo marsh where the *pili* grasses grew tall, to collect new thatching for his roof. When he reached the wide green field he strolled slowly, gazing out over the open expanse of luminous grasses. They billowed gently in the breeze, tickling his outstretched palms, and Kapoʻi could hear the grasses whisper softly to him, "Kapoʻi, you have come!" It was one of his favorite places. He smiled and began his task of gathering the sturdy leaves. Then he tied them up in tight bundles and started toward home.

But then Kapoʻi stopped abruptly, his keen eyes catching a glimpse of something hidden within the grasses. There on the ground before him lay the nest of an owl. Loosely constructed of grass and feathers, it held more than half a dozen eggs. *"Aia hoʻi!"* he exclaimed. "Look at this! What a delicious meal I will have!" Kneeling down, he gently grasped a single egg with the tips of his fingers and examined it closely. It seemed to glow and emanate warmth from its very center.

The sun was past its zenith and shadows began to fall all around. Kapoʻi knew that the mother owl was probably hunting nearby in these fields full of small prey and would be back to her nest before long. Kapoʻi worked quickly now, plucking up each egg with care and placing it in his small gourd container, cushioned by loose strands of grass. When he was finished, he had collected seven eggs in all.

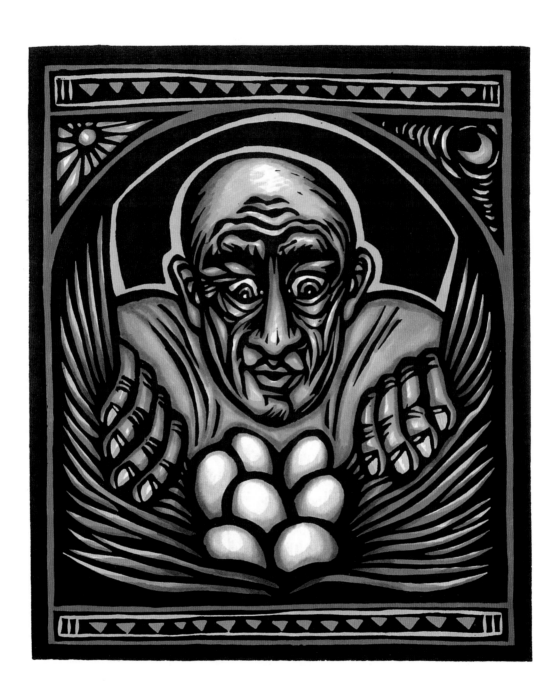

Kapoʻi arrived at his house and stowed away the gourd container, getting right to work on repairing his roof. He worked for the remainder of the day, and when night came he lay down on his bed of soft plaited mats, tired and content.

With his roof now sturdy and secure above him, he mused sleepily over the eggs and how he would prepare them in the morning. In his mind, he pictured how he would start a fire with his fire plow. Then, while the firewood was burning, he would wrap each of the seven eggs in *ti* leaves and broil them in the hot ashes. Happy with thoughts of the delicious meal he would soon be eating, he fell asleep.

In the middle of the night, Kapoʻi was awakened by a strange dream. In his dream, Pueo, the splendid owl, had the feathered body of a bird but the eyes of a human. Kapoʻi held in his mind the vivid, disturbing image of the mythic owl, staring at him with eyes full of wisdom. And then slumber overtook him.

When he opened his eyes again, it was to the soft, diffused light of morning. Warmed by the sun, the new *pili* grasses on the roof filled his small house with a sweet scent, and Kapoʻi breathed in deeply with pleasure. Then, remembering the eggs, he immediately rose to make a fire.

When he walked outside, Kapoʻi realized he was not alone. Sitting there on a branch of the *kou* tree growing just beside his house was an owl. Her huge golden eyes were fixed on Kapoʻi, and he suddenly remembered his dream from the night before. He tried not to appear concerned and crouched at his fire plow to start the fire, rubbing the hardwood stick into the groove. His hands fumbled with self-consciousness.

Then the owl spoke. "You have taken my eggs. Give them back to me."

Kapoʻi was surprised but told himself, "Oh, that voice I heard must have been the wind playing tricks on me." He ignored the owl and his nagging dream, and continued to work his stick in the fire plow's groove.

Pueo hopped to a branch that was closer to Kapoʻi. "Those eggs you have in your gourd container," said the owl, "they are mine. Now you must let me have them back."

Kapoʻi could not deny that the owl had spoken and stole a glance up to meet her unblinking stare. He noted her dignity and intelligence, and her sharp talons gripping the branch. Kapoʻi was a kind and perceptive man, but desire overshadowed his compassion and better judgment. He was still reluctant to part with the eggs.

He spoke to the owl with eyes averted. "So," he reasoned with her, "you say that the eggs are yours. Surely, then, you can tell me how many there are in all?"

Calmly, the majestic creature answered, "There are seven eggs, Kapoʻi, perfectly white, and each holds within it one of my future children. Now, will you please let me return them to the safety of my nest?"

Kapoʻi now looked fully at Pueo, who sat there, graceful and splendid. Watching him, she slowly opened her mighty wings to their full expanse, and each individual feather shimmered, seemingly painted by some invisible, meticulous stroke of a brush. Fine flecks of gold sparkled within her plumage. Kapoʻi caught his breath at her incredible beauty and power, and he suddenly felt a pained embarrassment at his attitude and actions. He realized now that this owl before him must be a god.

He hurried into his house, lifted the gourd that held the eggs, and brought it outside. He placed it before her and spoke with humility, prostrating himself on the ground. "Oh, Pueo, forgive me!" he murmured. "I did not know who you were. Please, take back your eggs and accept my apologies. No harm has come to them, I assure you!"

Pueo stared at Kapoʻi, the wisdom of all the world in her eyes. Finally, she spoke. "I forgive you, Kapoʻi. And now, I have something to ask of you. I would like you to build a *heiau*, a temple for me, in Mānoa Valley, and inside it place an altar with offerings of bananas and sacrifices. Dedicate the *heiau* and make the days that follow the dedication *kapu*, a time of prohibition. If you do all I ask of you, Kapo'i, then I will be your guardian spirit, your *'aumakua*. I will always protect and watch over you."

Feeling as though time had stopped, he nodded slowly. Then Pueo gathered up her eggs. Kapo'i watched, full of wonder and awe, as the owl took to the air on powerful wings. Once she was out of sight, Kapo'i immediately started on his way to Mānoa Valley, eager to build the *heiau* for his guardian.

Unknown to Kapo'i, Chief Kākuhihewa happened to have just built a new temple of his own, and at this time his subjects were all under *kapu*. Kākuhihewa had also made a declaration: Any new *heiau* built by his subjects could not be dedicated or placed under *kapu* until the ruler's own time of prohibition was lifted. If anyone were to break this law, he would be punished by death. When word reached Kākuhihewa of Kapo'i's temple, he considered this an act of rebellion. "Capture the builder of this *heiau*!" he shouted, and dispatched his men at once.

Kapo'i, of course, knew nothing of Kākuhihewa's new *heiau* or his new law. Oblivious to the approaching danger, Kapo'i sat with eyes closed inside his temple, praying quietly to Pueo. He did not even hear the sound of the men entering, so deep was his reverie.

Suddenly he felt his arms seized and his body being lifted roughly. The angry faces of Kākuhihewa's men shocked poor, terrified Kapo'i, who was mystified by their shouts of broken laws and his execution the next morning. As the men carried him toward the chief's compound, Kapo'i squinted upward, anxiously scanning the bright sky. And there he saw, gliding high above, his *'aumakua*, Pueo. As the owl flew away, Kapo'i felt deep in his heart a spark of hope.

Meanwhile, Pueo was flying fast and strong, seeking out the owls on every neighboring island. She flew from Hawai'i to Maui, Lāna'i to Moloka'i, Kaua'i, and all around O'ahu, gathering every owl to come and do battle against Chief Kākuhihewa of Waikīkī.

At daybreak, the sky over the compound was utterly black. Not a single ray of sunlight broke through the strange dark mass that hovered overhead, suspended in the air. A warrior looked up and felt terror in his belly as he recognized that this enormous cloud was made up of thousands of strong, feathered bodies and beating wings.

He rushed to the chief. "Chief Kākuhihewa!" he cried. "The sky is filled with owls! Thousands of owls! And I think they are preparing for battle! What shall we do?"

Chief Kākuhihewa scowled at the warrior. "Owls?" he said with derision. "You are afraid of owls? Surely you do not think they can harm us? The execution shall take place now!"

The guards lifted their prisoner by his arms and legs and carried him outside, and when the owls caught sight of Kapo'i, the attack began. Led by Pueo, they dove from the sky in a blaze of squawks, barks, hisses, and squeals. They ripped into the warriors with razor-sharp beaks and talons, beating at the men with mighty wings. The warriors tried to defend themselves, tried to fight back, but there were too many owls! They flew in spectacular aerial maneuvers, swooping, lunging, lashing, scratching, tearing at the flesh and testing the valor of every fighting man.

The battle was over quickly. Chief Kākuhihewa set Kapoʻi free at once, for he was bleeding and shaken, frightened by this strange, powerful enemy. The victorious owls flew off in all directions, like a great thundercloud dispersing, triumphantly singing, "VOO-HOO-HOO!" Chief Kākuhihewa then spoke to Kapoʻi and all of his subjects. With reverence, he said, "Kapoʻi, I am impressed with your god. I declare Pueo is a powerful god. I honor all the owls of these islands!" After this, owls became ʻaumākua to many people.

The scene of the battle in Waikīkī became known as Kūkaeunahiopueo, which means scaly excrement of owls, named for the offensive substance that the owls dropped all over their enemy during the battle. The locales around all the islands where the owls had gathered before going to fight were also given owl names. People were reminded of the battle of the owls when they passed through such places as Kalapueo, east of Diamond Head, Kanoniakapueo in Nuʻuanu Valley, and Pueohulunui, near Moanalua. To this day, these places still carry the memory of all the owls of Hawaiʻi and the great guardian protector, Pueo.

Kapoʻi was filled with gratitude and awe for his powerful and loving guardian. He continued to worship Pueo, leaving sacrifices at the *heiau* and saying prayers to her daily. He remembered how it all began, on that day long ago when he found those seven eggs that were to become the next generation of the mighty owl.

Under the Wings of Pueo

A MURKY, DENSE DARKNESS CONSUMED Ka'ili as he sat, hunched over in a damp corner of the *heiau*, against the temple wall. His wrists and ankles were chafed and raw from the rough *olonā* cords that bound him. Tied up so tightly, the boy could hardly move at all, and his poor body ached from being in the same cramped position for hours.

Kaʻili shuddered with terror and remorse. "*Auwē!*" he cried to himself in anguish. "I did not know!" But there was nothing he could do. As the guards slept on the other side of the high stone wall, the poor boy, in silent agony, went over and over again the events of the day, the choices he had made that brought him to this moment.

It had been a fine, sunny afternoon. Kaʻili and his sister, Nāʻilima, were walking along the hillside path above the sea, searching for a place where the boy could catch some fish for their evening meal. Waves crashed crisply against a reef surrounding a small, protected bay below, and Kaʻili stopped to look.

"Sister!" he said, "Look down there! Those clear, fresh waters invite me to come! I think in this bay I will have good luck with my net."

Nāʻilima looked down at the bay and smiled. "*E*, Kaʻili, you go. But do be careful!"

The boy climbed down the steep, rocky hill. When he reached the sandy shore, he found that the water was teeming with little fish. There were *pua ʻamaʻama*, baby striped mullet, *ʻiao*, silversides, *nehu*, anchovies, and *moiliʻi*, young threadfins.* Their swift silver bodies sparkled and gleamed in the shallow water like jewels. He lowered his net into the water with care, making sure to be quiet so as not to scare the small creatures away. "Come, you shining beauties!" he whispered. "Swim to me!"

Nāʻilima watched Kaʻili from high on the hill, leaning against the graceful trunk of a tall coconut palm tree. She studied her brother at work, noting his sharp eye and patient,

*In ancient times, the full-grown threadfin, *moi*, was a favorite fish of the chiefs, and commoners were forbidden to eat it.

deliberate movements with the net. Nāʻilima felt proud of him, for Kaʻili was a skillful fisherman.

The palm tree offered little shade, and Nāʻilima started feeling lazy and languid in the afternoon heat. Her eyelids grew heavy, and the hypnotic sounds of the surf below and chirping birds overhead lulled her into a sleepy trance. But suddenly a movement in the waters below caught her attention, jarring her awake.

A canoe had entered the bay, seemingly from out of nowhere. Led by a *kahuna*, the boat was being paddled furiously toward her brother, who had turned to the shore to empty his net, oblivious to their swift approach. "Kaʻili must have accidentally caught some fish that are *kapu*, sacred!" she cried, and knew at once that her brother was in grave danger.

"Ka'ili! Run!" she screamed, jumping to her feet, arms waving to get her brother's attention. But just as he looked up, they were upon him. The big men easily overpowered the startled boy, and they bound his hands and feet and tossed all the fish he had caught back into the sea. They threw Ka'ili into their canoe and paddled away, out of the bay and into the open sea.

Nā'ilima ran down the hillside path in terror, straining to keep the canoe in sight. She frantically called out to their family 'aumakua, "Pueo! Pueo, please come and help!" She cried and prayed, desperately repeating her earnest prayers again and again. And then, from out of the wide, brilliant blue sky, the great owl appeared.

He alighted soundlessly on a gnarled branch of a *wiliwili* tree growing next to the path. Nā'ilima stopped before him. He was beautiful and majestic, with his sleek torso and grand feathered wings tensed and ready for flight. With unblinking, intelligent eyes on Nā'ilima, he listened.

"Ē, Pueo!" she said quickly. "My brother, Ka'ili, was fishing in the bay when the *kahuna* came in a canoe with his men and captured him. We did not know these waters were sacred! Please, Pueo, help my brother! I am afraid he will be killed!"

The distant canoe was barely visible on the horizon now, but with his keen eyesight the owl could clearly see the boat and its occupants. Then, Nā'ilima watched as Pueo took to the air with a great rush of wind, flying swiftly to her brother.

The owl flew high in the sky along the shoreline, following the canoe. By the time the men brought the vessel to shore, the sun had almost set. In the growing darkness, Pueo kept watch as the *kahuna* and his men threw their prisoner inside the *heiau*. They finally settled down, leaning heavily against the outside wall of the temple. The owl waited, his sharp eyes on the men, whose breathing was growing slow with sleep.

And so there lay poor Kaʻili, still huddled in a miserable heap in the corner of the *heiau*, still wishing passionately that he had never used his net in those sacred waters. Pueo glided down soundlessly on outstretched wings, landing next to the boy. Kaʻili felt the stir of the air and turned his head slowly, fearful of what he might find. When he saw the owl, his family guardian, he was filled with joy.

"Pueo!" he whispered, but the owl looked hard at the boy, and Kaʻili realized he must be quiet. Ripping with his sharp talons and beak at the *olonā* cords that bound the boy's hands and feet, Pueo set Kaʻili free. The boy sprang to his feet, ignoring his stiff, sore limbs. He quickly scaled the temple wall opposite where the guards slept and, making not a sound,

jumped to the ground below. But when Kaʻili tried to run, the owl struck at him with powerful wings. Again and again the owl stopped the boy from running, until somehow Kaʻili understood that Pueo wanted him to walk backward.

The going was slow and awkward. The frustrated boy was terrified that he would be captured again, and the owl flew close by, stifling any attempts he made to turn and run forward. Kaʻili realized then that his trust in Pueo, his ʻaumakua, was absolute. He must obey. The men were now awake, their distant shouts getting closer, and Kaʻili could make out the glow of their kukui torches as they wound up the path, quickly gaining on him. With his guardian hovering protectively above him, the boy resolved to focus on his difficult task and overcome the paralyzing fear that gripped him.

Meanwhile, Nāʻilima waited anxiously at the top of the hill, her eyes on the path, with the pounding of the ocean below echoing the beating of her heart. When she finally saw her brother, Pueo flitting just above him, she called quietly. "Kaʻili! Over here! Hide behind this rock!"

He made his way carefully over to her and crouched behind the giant rock. Pueo flew down and beat a fierce wind with his wings, blowing away all traces of the boy's final steps, then flew up to a branch above them.

Nāʻilima sat against the rock, collecting herself, seconds before the angry men appeared. Breathing hard with exertion and fury, one of the men saw the girl and asked her, "Have you seen a boy run by this way?" She looked up at the man, composed and unconcerned, and said, "I have seen no one."

Just then, one of the men brought his torch close to the ground, catching sight of one of the footprints on the path. "Look!" he said, pointing down. "These footprints are fresh, and I am certain that they belong to our prisoner. They go the other way. He must have turned around and slipped by us, but

we can corner him by the sea. Follow me!" The men, with
their torches held low, rushed along the dark trail, following
Ka'ili's footprints back toward their *heiau*.

As soon as the torchlight had faded, Ka'ili and Nā'ilima
slipped away, dashing in the opposite direction, down the path
toward their home. Once they were a safe distance from the
men and the *kukui* torches could be seen no more, the brother
and sister hugged excitedly.

"My brother! I thought I would never see you again!" said
Nā'ilima breathlessly. She held him, and they pressed their
noses together affectionately. The boy looked up into the sky
and a huge smile spread across his face. "Look, sister," he cried,
pointing excitedly. "It is our Pueo!" They watched the owl
gliding high in the sky above and spoke of their love and
gratitude for Pueo, their marvelous, clever guardian, who had
saved Ka'ili from a certain death.

Then Ka'ili and Nā'ilima started on their way again,
dashing the rest of the way home, quiet and happy under the
protective wings of Pueo.

Notes on the Pueo

The word *pueo* in Hawaiian means owl. Called *Asio flammeus sandwichensis* by ornithologists, the bird's common name is the Hawaiian short-eared owl, because its earlike tufts are so small they are barely visible. The *pueo* is endemic to Hawai'i, and can be found nowhere else in the world. Unlike most owls, the *pueo* is diurnal and sleeps at night, hunting for small rodents in grassy fields and marshes by day. Because they fly so high, these owls may be mistaken for the 'io, the Hawaiian hawk, though the *pueo* is often seen in the evening, soundlessly gliding close to the ground. The owls build their nests on the ground in grassy areas, which makes their eggs and young vulnerable to predators. On O'ahu the *pueo* is endangered, primarily due to loss of habitat, and state and federal laws protect them.

Pueo, one of the oldest known guardian spirits, was protector to a great number of people in the ancient Hawaiian world. In the mid-1800s Isaac Kihe, a *kahuna*, or priest, from North Kona said that Pueo was "the most famous of all *'aumākua* to help." There are many historic accounts of indispensable aid given to worshippers, including early stories of the mighty owl rescuing lost souls on the plain from the dark realm of Po, the underworld, bringing them back to their bodies and to life. The great god Kāne was known to take on the guise of an owl and fight in battles to protect his people. Pueo freed prisoners, hid fugitives, and led whole armies to safety. In battle, an *ali'i*, or chief, would look to the owl for guidance, and wherever the bird alighted would be interpreted as a safe passage.

Hawaiians whose *'aumakua* is Pueo look at an owl not just as a powerful, graceful bird flying overhead. They observe the owl's pattern of flight and behavior meticulously, for clues may be hidden and guidance given in the wave of a wing or flick of the tail feathers. These are not the random actions of a wild animal. Instead, as the legends reveal, a god or the spirit of an ancestor may be alive within.

ABOUT THE
BLOCK PRINTS

The block prints appearing in this book were created using a basic technique that developed independently in many cultures. In fact, ancient Hawaiians invented a kind of block printing to decorate their *kapa,* or bark cloth. Highly skilled women practiced this refined and beautiful art form using stamps made from bamboo strips called *'ohe kapala.* The designs cut into the strips included a wide variety of geometrical motifs and straight lines. Colored dyes used to ink the stamps were made from the leaves, fruit, bark, nuts, roots, tubers, berries, and flowers of local plants. The repeating patterns were pressed down on the cloth, either over a large area or only along the edges, as a border. While bark cloth has been produced throughout Polynesia, this form of block printing on *kapa* was unique to Hawai'i.

Growing up, I was lucky to have a mother who was a prolific artist and teacher. We spent summer days at the beach—my mother making woodcuts while my brother and I played. I loved watching her strong hands work the tools, the metal blade gouging out thin lines of wood, and I would collect the curly strands left in the sand. I could spend hours this way without getting bored, because it was fascinating to see the image as it was gradually revealed. My own block carving methods have developed mostly through experimentation, but luckily I have my mother to call on whenever I have a question or a problem.

When I make a block print, I do a lot of work before I even touch the block. First, I research the legends and Hawaiian natural history, so I can represent the plants, animals, and life in ancient Hawai'i as accurately as possible. I attempt to bring forth the essence of the plant or animal, those qualities that might suggest the spirit within. This results in a symbolic portrayal of the story sometimes and a literal depiction at other times. I also enjoy weaving elements from the legend into the borders as decorative details.

I spend a great deal of time developing my drawing on paper and do not transfer the image to the block until I am satisfied with the design. All cuts are permanent, and I have learned to my frustration that when a cut is made by accident, the block is ruined. So I am certain of every line before I do any carving.

All areas that will appear white on the finished print are carved out of the block's surface. The prints appearing in this volume were made with rubber or linoleum blocks. While a variety of specialized tools are available for carving, my favorite is a simple mat knife with a fresh, sharp blade.

The printing is the most exciting part of the process—it's the "grand finale" and always a surprise. I apply ink to the block with a roller, so that it covers the uncut surfaces. I carefully lay paper over the inked block, then rub the entire surface evenly with a wooden spoon. In a moment of tension and anticipation, I pull the paper slowly off the block and the

final image is revealed. The colored images in this book all began as black-and-white prints, which I painted with washes of ink. Any translucent medium will do, such as watercolor paints, drawing inks applied with a brush, or artist's markers.

Block printing is a very pleasing medium with which to work. I enjoy its simplicity and its roots in ancient history, and it is gratifying to continue the work that my mother taught me by example. Although the results are sometimes disappointing and I have to go "back to the drawing board," I am almost always happily surprised. The animals and plants I have studied and the legends I love so very much now have a life of their own in the dancing lines and shapes that sweep across the printed page.

GENERAL SOURCES

Baybayan, Chad. "Traditional Foods and Their Preparation."
    Polynesian Voyaging Society. 12 Mar. 2001
    <http://pvs.hawaii.org/ancientprovisions.html>.
Baybayan, Chad, Rowena Keaka, Melissa Kim, Beatrice
    Krauss, and Mollie Sperry. "Plants Used for Building
    Canoes." *Polynesian Voyaging Society*. 14 Mar. 2001
    <http://pvs.hawaii.org/buildplants.html>.
Beckwith, Martha. Aumakua Stories. M. W. Beckwith
    Collection of Notes, Hawaiian Ethnographical Notes I,
    Bishop Museum Library Archives, Honolulu, ca. 1934.
    1439–1454.
———. *Hawaiian Mythology*. Honolulu: University of Hawai'i
    Press, 1970. (Originally published in 1940.)
———. The Owl God. (Told by a native of Waipio Valley.)
    M. W. Beckwith Collection of Notes, Hawaiian
    Ethnographical Notes I, Bishop Museum Library
    Archives, Honolulu, ca. 1934. 1456–1457.
———. Puhi. M. W. Beckwith Collection of Notes, Hawaiian
    Ethnographical Notes I, Bishop Museum Library Archives,
    Honolulu, ca. 1934. 1386–1387.
Beckwith, Martha W., ed. *The Kumulipo: A Hawaiian Creation
    Chant*. Honolulu: University of Hawai'i Press, 1994.
    (Originally published in 1951.)
Boom, Robert. *Hawaiian Seashells*. Honolulu: Boom
    Enterprises, 1972.
Bringham, William Tufts. The Ancient Worship of the
    Hawaiian Islanders with Reference to that of other
    Polynesians. Manuscript, Bishop Museum Library
    Archives, Honolulu, Special Collections, ca. 1889.
Colver, Kevin. "Pacific Golden Plover." *eNature.com, Living
    Nature Audio*, 23 July 2001 <http://www.enature.com/
    guides/play_bird_real.asp?recnum=BD0660>.

Ekaula, Samuela. What are Aumakuas in the Beliefs of the Ancients. *Ancient Worship*. From *Ka Nupepa Kuokoa*. Trans. T. G. Thrum. Hawaiian Ethnographical Notes #28, Thrum Collection, Bishop Museum Library Archives, Honolulu, 1865.

Emerson, Joseph S. "The Lesser Hawaiian Gods." *Hawaiian Historical Society Papers*. No. 2: 1–24. Honolulu, 1892.

Emory, Kenneth P. "Isles of the Pacific I: The Coming of the Polynesians." *National Geographic*, 146.6 (Dec. 1974): 732–745.

Fornander, Abraham. Fornander collection of Hawaiian antiquities and folk-lore. Ed. T. G. Thrum. Trans. John Wise. *Memoirs of the Bernice Pauahi Bishop Museum, 1916–20*. Vols. 4–6. Honolulu.

Forrest, Peter. "An Encounter with the Pueo of Hawaii." *The Owl Pages*. 26 Nov. 1998. 15 Jan. 2001 <http://www.owlpages.com/articles/pueo.htm>.

Goodson, Gar. *The Many-Splendored Fishes of Hawaii*. Stanford, CA: Stanford University Press, 1991. (Originally published in 1985.)

Green, Laura. *Folktales from Hawaii, 2nd Series*. Ed. Martha Beckwith. Poughkeepsie, NY: Vassar College, 1926.

Gutmanis, June. *Kahuna Laʻau Lapaʻau: The Practice of Hawaiian Herbal Medicine*. Trans. Theodore Kelsey. Aiea, HI: Island Heritage Publishing, 1976.

Handy, E. S. Craighill. "Dreaming in Relation to Spirit Kindred and Sickness in Hawaiʻi." *Essays in Anthropology in Honor of Alfred Louis Kroebe*. Ed. R. H. Lowie. Berkeley: University of California Press, 1936.

Handy, E. S. Craighill, Elisabeth G. Handy, and Mary Kawena Pukui. *Native Planters in Old Hawaii: Their Life, Lore, and Environment*. Honolulu: Bernice P. Bishop Museum Bulletin 233, 1972.

Handy, E. S. Craighill, and Mary Kawena Pukui. *The Polynesian Family System in Ka-ʻu, Hawaiʻi*. Rutland, VT: Charles E. Tuttle, 1958.

Harden, M. J. *Voices of Wisdom: Hawaiian Elders Speak*. Kula, HI: Aka Press, 1999.

Hawai'i Heritage Program. "*Asio flammeus sandwichensis*, Common name: Hawaiian short-eared owl, *pueo*." 15 Jan. 2001 <http://www.abi.org/nhp/us/hi/pueo.htm>.

Henriques, Edgar. "Hawaiian Canoes." *The 34th Annual Report of the Hawaiian Historical Society*. Honolulu, 1925. 15–19.

Holmes, Tommy. *The Hawaiian Canoe*, 2nd Edition. Honolulu: Editions Limited, 1993. (Originally published in 1981.)

Hoover, John. *Hawai'i's Sea Creatures: A Guide to Hawai'i's Marine Invertebrates*. Honolulu: Mutual Publishing, 1998.

Ii, John Papa. *Fragments of Hawaiian History*. Trans. Mary Kawena Pukui. Ed. Dorothy B. Barrère. Honolulu: Bishop Museum Press, 1959.

Kaaie, J. W. K. "The soul after leaving the Body." *Ka Hoku o Ka Pakipika* (newspaper), Hawaiian Ethnographical Notes #194, Thrum Collection, Bishop Museum Library Archives, Honolulu, 8 May 1862.

Kamakau, Samuel M. *Ka Po'e Kahiko: The People of Old*. Trans. Mary Kawena Pukui. Ed. Dorothy B. Barrère. Honolulu: Bernice P. Bishop Museum Special Publication 51, 1964.

———. *Na Hana a ka Po'e Kahiko: The Works of the People of Old*. Trans. Mary Kawena Pukui. Ed. Dorothy B. Barrère. Honolulu: Bernice P. Bishop Museum Special Publication 61, 1976.

———. *The Ruling Chiefs of Hawaii*. Honolulu: Kamehameha Schools Press, 1961.

———. *Tales and Traditions of the People of Old: Na Mo'olelo a ka Po'e Kahiko*. Trans. Mary Kawena Pukui. Ed. Dorothy B. Barrère. Honolulu: Bernice P. Bishop Museum Special Publication 94, 1993.

Kamali, Keliihue. The people of Kamaoa, Ka'ū. Legend of a Gourd. Hawaiian Ethnographical Notes #1099. Bishop Museum Library Archives, Honolulu, 1935.

Kane, Herb Kawainui. *Ancient Hawai'i*. Captain Cook, HI: The Kawainui Press, 1997.

———. "Evolution of the Hawaiian Canoe." *The Polynesian Voyaging Society*. 1998. 7 Mar. 2001 <http://pvs.hawaii.org/evolution.html>.

———. "Isles of the Pacific III: The Pathfinders." *National Geographic*, 146.6 (Dec. 1974): 756–761.

———. *Pele, Goddess of Hawai'i's Volcanoes*. Captain Cook, HI: The Kawainui Press, 1997.

———. *Voyagers: A Collection of Words and Images*. Captain Cook, HI: The WhaleSong Collection, 1991.

Kauhane. "The history of Kane, his power and his various works." *Ancient Worship*. Trans. T. G. Thrum (from *Ka Nupepa Kuokoa*). Hawaiian Ethnographical Notes #19, Thrum Collection, Bishop Museum Library Archives, Honolulu, 1865.

———. "The story of Ku, his character and his works." *Ancient Worship*. Trans. T. G. Thrum (from *Ka Nupepa Kuokoa*). Hawaiian Ethnographical Notes #20, Thrum Collection, Bishop Museum Library Archives, Honolulu, 1865.

Kawaharada, Dennis. "The Settlement of Polynesia, Part 1." *Polynesian Voyaging Society*. 7 Mar. 2001 <http://pvs.hawaii.org/migrationspart1.html>.

———. "The Settlement of Polynesia, Part 2." *Polynesian Voyaging Society*. 7 Mar. 2001 <http://pvs.hawaii.org/migrationspart2.html>.

———. "Wayfinding, or Non-Instrument Navigation." *Polynesian Voyaging Society*. 7 Mar. 2001 <http://pvs.hawaii.org/navigate/navigate.html>.

Kepelino, K. *Kepelino's traditions of Hawaii*. Ed. Martha Beckwith. Honolulu: Bernice P. Bishop Museum Bulletin 95, 1932.

Kihe, Isaac. Notes on "Aumakuas." J. S. Emerson's collection. Typescript in Hawaiian Ethnographical Notes, Bishop Museum Library Archives, Honolulu, ca. 1850. 1: 566–572.

Kirch, Patrick Vinton. *Feathered Gods and Fishhooks: An Introduction to Hawaiian Archaeology and Prehistory*. Honolulu: University of Hawai'i Press, 1995. (Originally published in 1985.)

Knudsen, Eric. *Teller of Hawaiian Tales*. Honolulu: Mutual Publishing, 1987. (Originally published in 1946.)

Lewis, David. "Isles of the Pacific II: Wind, Wave, Star and Bird." *National Geographic*, 146.6 (Dec. 1974): 747–778.

Lindo, Cecilia Kapua. "The Spirit of 'Ohana and the Polynesian Voyagers." *Polynesian Voyaging Society*. 7 Mar. 2001 <http://pvs.hawaii.org/migrationsohana.html>.

Lindo, Cecilia Kapua, and Nancy Alpert Mower, eds. *Polynesian Seafaring Heritage*. Honolulu: Kamehameha Schools and the Polynesian Voyaging Society, 1980.

Malo, David. *Hawaiian Antiquities: Mo'olelo Hawai'i*. Trans. Nathaniel B. Emerson. Honolulu: Bernice P. Bishop Museum Special Publication 2, 1951. (Originally published in 1903.)

Manu, Moke, et al. *Hawaiian Fishing Traditions*. Ed. Dennis Kawaharada. Honolulu: Kalamakū Press, 1992.

Miller, Debbie. *Flight of the Golden Plover: The Amazing Migration Between Hawaii and Alaska*. Anchorage: Alaska Northwest Books, 1996.

Miyano, Leland, and Douglas Peebles. *Hawai'i's Beautiful Trees*. Honolulu: Mutual Publishing, 1997.

Morton, Julia F. "Breadfruit." *Fruits of Warm Climates*. 24 Oct. 2001 <http://newcrop.hort.purdue.edu/newcrop/morton/breadfruit.html>.

Mulroney, Merryl. *Treasures of the Rainforest: An Introduction to the Endangered Forest Birds of Hawai'i*. Volcano, HI: The Peregrine Fund, 1999.

Nakuina, Emma M., et al. *Nanaue the Shark Man and Other Hawaiian Shark Stories*. Ed. Dennis Kawaharada. Honolulu: Kalamakū Press, 1994.

Nimmo, H. Arlo. *The Pele Literature: An Annotated Bibliography of the English-Language Literature on Pele, Volcano Goddess of Hawai'i*. Honolulu: Bernice P. Bishop Museum Bulletin in Anthropology 4, 1992.

Owl Pages. "Short-eared Owls—*Asio flammeus*." 1 Jan. 2001 <http://www.owlpages.com/species/asio/flammeus/default.htm>.

Padraic, Colum. *Legends of Hawai'i*. New Haven, CT: Yale University Press, 1937.

Parker, Steve, and Jane Parker. *The Encyclopedia of Sharks*. Buffalo: Firefly Books, 1999.

Polynesian Voyaging Society. "Dangers at Sea." 12 Mar. 2001 <http://pvs.hawaii.org/lifedangers.html>.

———. "Fish, Birds, and Mammals of the Open Ocean." 12 Mar. 2001 <http://pvs.hawaii.org/rapanui/sealife.html>.

———. "Hawaiian Deities of Canoes and Canoe Building." 14 Mar. 2001 <http://pvs.hawaii.org/builddeities.html>.

———. "Parts of the Hawaiian Canoe." 14 Mar. 2001 <http://pvs.hawaii.org/buildparts.html>.

Pratt, Douglas, and Jack Jeffrey. *A Pocket Guide to Hawai'i's Birds*. Honolulu: Mutual Publishing, 1996.

Pukui, Mary Kawena, trans. *Nā Mele Welo, Songs of our Heritage: Selections from the Roberts Mele Collection in Bishop Museum, Honolulu*. Ed. Pat Namaka Bacon and Nathan Napoka. Honolulu: Bernice P. Bishop Museum Special Publication 88, 1995.

———, trans. *'Ōlelo No'eau: Hawaiian Proverbs and Poetical Sayings*. Honolulu: Bernice P. Bishop Museum Special Publication 71, 1983.

Pukui, Mary Kawena, and Caroline Curtis. *Hawai'i Island Legends: Pīkoi, Pele and Others*. Honolulu: Kamehameha Schools Press, 1996. (Originally published in 1949.)

———. *The Water of Kāne and Other Legends of the Hawaiian Islands*. Honolulu: Kamehameha Schools Press, 1995. (Originally published in 1951.)

Pukui, Mary Kawena, and Samuel H. Elbert. *The New Pocket Hawaiian Dictionary*. Honolulu: University of Hawai'i Press, 1992. (Originally published in 1975.)

Pukui, Mary Kawena, Samuel H. Elbert, and Esther T. Mookini. *Pocket Place Names of Hawai'i*. Honolulu: University of Hawai'i Press, 1966.

Pukui, Mary Kawena, trans., and Laura C. S. Green. *Folktales of Hawai'i. He Mau Ka'ao Hawai'i*. Honolulu: Bernice P. Bishop Museum Special Publication 87, 1995.

Ramirez, Tino. "Sharks: An ocean dilemma." *Honolulu Advertiser* (19 Sep. 1993): A1.

Randall, John. *Shore Fishes of Hawai'i*. Honolulu: University of Hawai'i Press, 1998.

St. John, Harold, and Kuaika Jendrusch. "Plants Introduced to Hawai'i by the Ancestors of the Hawaiian People." *Polynesian Voyaging Society*. 7 Mar. 2001 <http://pvs.hawaii.org/migrationsplants.html>.

Suzumoto, Arnold. *Sharks Hawai'i*. Honolulu: Bishop Museum Press, 1991.

Te Rangi Hiroa (Peter H. Buck). *Arts and Crafts of Hawaii*. Sections 1–13. Honolulu: Bernice P. Bishop Museum Special Publication 45, 1957.

Thompson, Nainoa. "Nainoa Thompson and the Lost Art of Polynesian Navigation: Hokulea—Navigators, Primitive." *Oceans*, 21.4 (1988): 16–24.

Thrum, Thomas G., ed. *Hawaiian Folk Tales: A Collection of Native Legends*. Honolulu: Mutual Publishing, 1998. (Originally published in 1907.)

————. *More Hawaiian Folk Tales*. Chicago: McClurg, 1923.

Titcomb, Margaret. *Native Use of Fish in Hawaii*. Honolulu: University of Hawai'i Press, 1995. (Originally published in 1952.)

Valeri, Valerio. *Kingship and Sacrifice: Ritual and Society in Ancient Hawaii*. Trans. Paula Wissing. Chicago: University of Chicago Press, 1985.

Westervelt, William D. *Hawaiian Legends of Ghosts and Ghost Gods*. Honolulu: Mutual Publishing, 1998. (Originally published in 1915.)

————. *Myths and Legends of Hawai'i*. Honolulu: Mutual Publishing, 1987. (Originally published in 1913.)

Williams, Julie Stewart. *From the Mountains to the Sea: Early Hawaiian Life*. Honolulu: Kamehameha Schools Press, 1997.

LEGEND SOURCES

The legends in this volume were adapted from the following sources.

THE GIFT OF KŪ

Beckwith, Martha. *Hawaiian Mythology*. Honolulu: University of Hawai'i Press, 1970. (Originally published in 1940.) 98.

Handy, E. S. Craighill, Elisabeth G. Handy, and Mary Kawena Pukui. *Native Planters in Old Hawaii: Their Life, Lore, and Environment*. 151.

Handy, E. S. Craighill, and Mary Kawena Pukui. *The Polynesian Family System in Ka-'u, Hawai'i*. 33.

Pukui, Mary Kawena, and Caroline Curtis. *Hawai'i Island Legends: Pīkoi, Pele and Others*. Honolulu: Kamehameha Schools Press, 1996. (Originally published in 1949.) 176.

Pukui, Mary Kawena, trans., and Laura C. S. Green. *Folktales of Hawai'i. He Mau Ka'ao Hawai'i*. 8.

Te Rangi Hiroa (Peter H. Buck). *Arts and Crafts of Hawaii, Section One, Food*. 8.

THE SACRED TREE

Beckwith, Martha. *Hawaiian Mythology*. Honolulu: University of Hawai'i Press, 1970. (Originally published in 1940.) 281–283.

Pukui, Mary Kawena, and Caroline Curtis. *The Water of Kāne and Other Legends of the Hawaiian Islands*. Honolulu: Kamehameha Schools Press, 1995. (Originally published in 1951.) 136, 137.

Westervelt, William D. *Myths and Legends of Hawai'i*. Honolulu: Mutual Publishing, 1987. (Originally published in 1913.) 181–186.

A WARNING FROM THE GOD OF THE PLOVER

Beckwith, Martha. *Hawaiian Mythology*. Honolulu: University of Hawai'i Press, 1970. (Originally published in 1940.) 137, 138.

Green, Laura. *Folktales from Hawaii, 2nd Series*. Ed. Martha Beckwith. (As told by Mrs. Wiggin.) 1926. 108–110.

Pukui, Mary Kawena, trans., and Laura C. S. Green. *Folktales of Hawai'i. He Mau Ka'ao Hawai'i*. (As told by Mrs. Wiggin.) Honolulu: Bishop Museum Press, 1995. 64–67.

LEGEND OF THE LITTLE GREEN SHARK

Beckwith, Martha. Aumakua Stories. M. W. Beckwith Collection of Notes, Hawaiian Ethnographical Notes 1, Bishop Museum Library Archives, Honolulu, ca. 1934. 1439–1454.

———. *Hawaiian Mythology*. Honolulu: University of Hawai'i Press, 1970. (Originally published in 1940.) 132, 133.

———. Puhi. M. W. Beckwith Collection of Notes, Hawaiian Ethnographical Notes 1, Bishop Museum Library Archives, Honolulu, ca. 1934. 1386–1387.

Handy, E. S. Craighill, and Mary Kawena Pukui. *Polynesian Family System in Ka-'u, Hawai'i*. 1958. 35–37.

TWINS OF THE GOURD

Beckwith, Martha. *Hawaiian Mythology*. Honolulu: University of Hawai'i Press, 1970. (Originally published in 1940.) 98, 99.

Handy, E. S. Craighill, Elisabeth G. Handy, and Mary Kawena Pukui. *Native Planters in Old Hawaii: Their Life, Lore, and Environment*. Honolulu: Bishop Museum Press, 1972. 218, 219, 582, 583.

Handy, E. S. Craighill, and Mary Kawena Pukui. *Polynesian Family System in Ka-'u, Hawai'i*. 38, 39.

Kamali, Keliihue. The people of Kamaoa, Ka'ū. Legend of a Gourd. Hawaiian Ethnographical Notes #1099. Bishop Museum Library Archives, Honolulu, 1935.

Pukui, Mary Kawena, trans., and Laura C. S. Green. *Folktales of Hawai'i. He Mau Ka'ao Hawai'i.* (As told by Ka'ehuokekai McGiffen.) Honolulu: Bishop Museum Press, 1995. 62, 63.

THE SEVEN EGGS

Beckwith, Martha. *Hawaiian Mythology.* Honolulu: University of Hawai'i Press, 1970. (Originally published in 1940.) 124, 125.

Kamakau, Samuel M. *Tales and Traditions of the People of Old: Na Mo'olelo a ka Po'e Kahiko.* Trans. Mary Kawena Pukui. Ed. Dorothy B. Barrère. Honolulu: Bishop Museum Press, 1993. 23.

Knudsen, Eric. *Teller of Hawaiian Tales.* Honolulu: Mutual Publishing, 1987. (Originally published in 1946.) 27–29.

Thrum, Thomas G., ed. *Hawaiian Folk Tales: A Collection of Native Legends.* (As told by Jos. M. Poepoe.) 1907. 200–202.

Westervelt, William D. *Myths and Legends of Hawai'i.* Honolulu: Mutual Publishing, 1987. (Originally published in 1913.) 228–230.

UNDER THE WINGS OF PUEO

Pukui, Mary Kawena, and Caroline Curtis. *The Water of Kāne and Other Legends of the Hawaiian Islands.* Honolulu: Kamehameha Schools Press, 1995. (Originally published in 1951.) 190–193.